The Butcher's
TALE

The Butcher's TALE

AND OTHER STORIES

DEREK UPDEGRAFF

Stephen F. Austin State University Press

For more information:
Stephen F. Austin State University Press
P.O. Box 13007 SFA Station
Nacogdoches, Texas 75962
sfapress@sfasu.edu
www.sfasu.edu/sfapress

Book design: Shaina Hawkins
Cover design: Shaina Hawkins
Cover art: Jonathan Apgar
Distrubted by Texas A&M Consortium
www.tamupress.com

LIBRARY OF CONGRESS CATALOGING-IN-PUBLICATION DATA
Updegraff, Derek
The Butcher's Tale and Other Stories/ Derek Updegraff
ISBN: 978-1-62288-128-4

for Elizabeth

contents

a small, distant thing

The inside of the bar wasn't as dim as the outside suggested, with its spot off the Branson strip, tucked behind the shadows of the family theaters and illuminated only by the red glow of its sign. Courtney took another sip of her cabernet. She had hesitated when taking the first sip, and Tanner had looked puzzled, or perhaps concerned, when she held the glass just out of her lips' reach, keeping it there for many seconds as she studied the once-dark maroon made bright by the light above their table. But his face relaxed when she took a sip and answered his question. I'm not too hungry, she had said. Perhaps we can order food back at the hotel. So they sat there, at a four-top booth, and the light was bright, and Tanner was finishing his second beer while Courtney attended to her first glass, drinking without hesitation but still with slowness as she brought the rim forward, each time tilting the glass back just so but allowing only the slightest bit to glide past her lips and into her mouth.

The waitress made her way back through the tables in the center of the room and over toward their booth along the far wall. Behind the waitress, the bar singer was getting ready to sing again, fiddling with her cordless microphone while making small talk with a couple at a two-top in the middle of the room, having returned from a break that lasted only a few minutes. When Courtney and Tanner first entered the bar, the singer was halfway through Sinatra's "These Boots Are Made for Walkin'," and then she sang two other numbers that Courtney didn't recognize. But most of the other patrons seemed to know them as they chimed along and sang a verse or two

1

into the microphone whenever the singer held it out before them, offering it briefly before pulling it back and letting her own voice reclaim the air. And she was right to do that, Courtney had thought. Her voice was sweet and strong, and this was her moment. The singer's name was Hope. Hope Mattison. Courtney had caught the name on a pile of CDs stacked next to a register near the front entrance. The CDs looked home-produced, and Courtney had planned on buying one before they left.

The waitress reached their booth, and while she stood there she placed her hands on the table and leaned in toward them. Her breasts became taut each time she'd done this, but Courtney didn't mind. The waitress was friendly and reminded her of a more seasoned version of a close college friend she'd lost touch with in recent years. Tanner could have a look if he wanted. But he hadn't yet, and Courtney appreciated his restraint.

"Another beer?" said the waitress.

"Please," Tanner said. "And another cab sav too."

The waitress faced Courtney. "You ready for another?" she said.

Courtney examined her glass. It was less than a third full. "Sure," she said. "But then that's it for me."

"House cab still good?"

"That's fine," said Courtney.

"Sounds good," said the waitress, who turned and headed back to the bar.

The house cabernet was from some local winery in southern Missouri. Courtney took another sip from her first glass. It was good. And then for the first time that night she thought that she would make it her new wine of choice when she moved back there.

The waitress returned with the drinks and set them on the table, and then she put the bill down too, in the center, evenly between each drink, and said that it would be no worries to add more to the tab. She'd printed it out for their convenience. That's all. They were welcome to stay as long as they'd like. She'd be happy to add more drinks to the tab and would still keep checking on them, she'd said.

Courtney and Tanner had spent the first minutes in the booth discussing their day in Branson, but then they sat quietly for much of the time. The trip was beginning to wear on them, and Courtney, usually the most talkative of the pair, was herself more preoccupied than usual.

Then she tapped his hand with a finger, and he looked up from his glass, and she brought her own hand back and asked, "How's your beer, anyway?"

"It's okay," he said. "Guinness tastes flat to me these days. It's tough for me to get into it."

"Maybe their keg's old."

"I wouldn't doubt it. But it's not that. I still make the mistake of buying it in the grocery store now and then. I remember it with fondness. But then I'm always disappointed. It's a flat beer." Tanner tilted his glass toward himself and let the dark liquid slide down near the brim before leveling it out again. "It's funny because I always remember it being a stout beer, you know? I think of it as being tough to get down. Not difficult, mind you. But heavy as it slides down the throat. Having flavor. Like a Bully Porter or a 1554. But it's more like the pisswater beers they've got on tap here."

"I'm sorry they didn't have it."

Tanner finished off the last sip of his second drink and set the glass back on the table. A thin line of foam encircled the inside wall of the glass, and a remaining droplet of the beer slid down the outside wall facing him. He pushed the empty glass aside and slid the new one closer.

"The Bully Porter, I mean. I'm sorry they didn't have it. Or anything else dark."

"I know, right? It's local and all. But this is their only dark option."

"It's not really local," she said.

"It's from Kansas City."

"I know. But that's not anywhere near here."

"Same state. Right? A hell of a lot closer than the Long Beach grocery store I buy it from."

Courtney didn't say anything.

Tanner seemed to understand that he was getting worked up over nothing. "I'm sorry," he said. "How are you doing? That's what I want to know. Are you still okay with all of this? Have you been thinking about your aunt at all?"

It was early in the morning when Courtney discovered that she was pregnant. She slipped out in the gray light and bought a test while Tanner slept, and then she took it in their hotel bathroom and disposed of it in the hallway trash can farthest away. When she got back to their room, she took her laptop into the bathroom and researched the situation online. They'd

3

had drinks each night since the funeral two days ago, and she knew that Tanner wanted to go out that night, to try to find some dive on their last night in Branson. All the websites told her not to worry about the drinks. So you've just discovered that you're pregnant, they said, but you've had some drinks in the first days while you didn't know. It's okay, they said. There's no research linking any problems to having had some drinks at the onset of the pregnancy. But now you need to stop, of course. Of course, now that you know, they all said, it is time to stop.

He had been sweet to her throughout the day. They'd toured the Country Boulevard strip some more and took in two shows along with the wax museum. They'd photographed each other in the museum—her beside Johnny Depp, him beside Marilyn Monroe—and they walked among the displays holding hands as they did in their first days of dating, admitting to each other an affinity toward the still figures, a kind of smugness since they too were from southern California. Later she reminded him that she had grown up there—in the south of Missouri, not Branson but east of there in the small town of Willow Springs. It doesn't matter, he'd said. You were what? Six, seven, when you left? Look around. This has to be a trip for you too. I mean, get a load of these people, he'd said. And it *was* an odd sight to her as well. All that country glitz. But this was Branson. It was like no place else she'd ever seen. And the tourists were from all across the Midwest and the South. It wasn't Missouri they were taking in. It was something else. And she did remember those last years here. She remembered the roughness of her grandpa's hands. And she remembered seeing her grandpa shake the hand of her mom's then-boyfriend, saying to his daughter and granddaughter after the boyfriend had left that he—that *that boy*, as he'd said—was all hat and no cattle.

Courtney stared up at Tanner and wondered if her grandpa would say the same thing about him if they could meet. "I barely knew her," said Courtney. "I hadn't seen my aunt or anyone else since my mom moved us away."

"It's too bad," said Tanner. "Those were nice things everyone said about her. And about your mom too. People kept telling me how sorry they were that she couldn't make it out."

"Yeah," said Courtney.

"But they were all so happy to see you," said Tanner. "People kept telling me, 'It's so great Courtney's here. It was so thoughtful of her to make it out for this.'"

"Thoughtful?"

"Yeah," said Tanner. "I've been telling you. They thought it was thoughtful of you."

"You said 'responsible' yesterday."

"Exactly."

"So which was it?" said Courtney.

"I don't know," said Tanner. "Both, I think. I think I heard different people saying each. One person would say, 'Look, there's Courtney. It's very responsible of her to come.' And then another—an uncle, a cousin, God-knows-who, there were so many of them, you know—then another would say, 'There's Trish's daughter. How thoughtful of her to be here.'"

"It doesn't matter," Courtney said. "Let's talk about something else. I still don't want to talk about that. Okay," she said. "Let's talk about this bar. Let's talk about Hope Mattison. Anything, okay?"

"Sure," said Tanner. He took a sip from his new glass, and she took a sip from her first one, finishing off the last of it, and then they each set their glasses down and Tanner said, "Who's Hope Mattison?"

"The singer."

"Which singer?"

Courtney nodded toward the center of the room, where Hope meandered through the tables, singing another country number she didn't recognize. "That singer," she said.

The bar continued to fill. Most of the tables in the center were occupied. Fewer people chose to sit in the booths lining the two back walls. Waitresses brought pitchers and appetizers to the tables, and Hope kept the place energized, visiting table after table, resting a hand on this one's shoulder, shooting a smile to that one before starting up the chorus again.

"How do you know her name is Hope?" said Tanner.

"It's on those CDs by the door."

"It sounds made up," he said.

"It's not," she said. "Look at her. There's nothing inauthentic about her."

"You don't think it's a stage name?"

"What stage?" said Courtney. "Those days are behind her. Or maybe she never had them. Maybe she never made it to the theaters. But I'm sure her name is Hope. It was her mother's choice. Her parents had selected another name. Mary, or maybe Nancy. But then when she was born and the doctor handed her to her, the mother said that her name would be Hope. It came to her right then. In the delivery room. No other name but Hope would do."

Tanner took another sip of his beer and kept holding onto the glass after he'd set it back down. "And now." Tanner paused for a moment as he seemed to map out his next sentence before vocalizing it. "Now Hope is a middle-aged, still-attractive singer of others' songs in an off-the-strip bar in Branson."

"Yes."

"What do you call that?" said Tanner.

"A metaphor," said Courtney.

"No," he said. "That's not what I mean. That's not what I mean at all. You're always doing that," he said. "Who the hell knows what a metaphor is but you? You know what I mean to say."

Courtney took a small sip of her wine and then set the glass back down.

"That it's bad luck," he said. "Or that she was supposed to be better than this."

The pair quieted, each staring off at Hope as she strolled through the maze of occupied chairs close to the bar's edge. Courtney thought about Hope's childhood. She thought about the boys who called her house only to get the mother on the line. Hope isn't here, the mother would say. Hope is in the backyard helping her brothers. Hope is in the shower. Hope is doing her homework. Hope is busy. Try again, the mother would say. Hope is busy now.

"Hope is busy," Courtney said. "That's what her mom had to say when she was a girl and someone called for her and she couldn't come to the phone."

"Another metaphor," said Tanner.

She didn't want to correct him, so she said, "Yes."

"I like it," he said. And then he said, "Do you think she's from here?"

But she remembered more than just her grandpa and his rough hands. She remembered the green of their lawns and the nearby woods. The green that sprang up as soon as the frosts were over. An electric green that took hold in the ground and branches and remained bright for more than half the year. That was one of the first things Tanner had said three days ago when they drove the rental car from Springfield to Branson, that it was really green there, that the green was almost electric. And Courtney had said that that was a nice phrase, that she had liked the description. But she didn't know then that she would want to move back there, that seeing all that green would make her remember the water too. All those streams and creeks, the float trips her family would congregate for, her and her grandpa sharing a canoe, him dragging it across the exposed pebbles in spots where the water was low, the sound of the metal bottom scraping against the rocks while she sat in the front of the boat, her grandpa tugging all the while. That was the type of water Courtney longed for now. Not the roar of the ocean's waves. Not the miles of concrete pressed up against a sliver of sand, parking lots and highways gesturing toward a blue horizon of an impossible expansiveness. But the murmur of all that water contained in its meanderings contained in a steady whisper beneath those green canopying trees—that's what she needed now. And now she looked at Tanner and answered his question. "She's from here," she said. "She grew up not far from here on her family's farm. They had cattle mostly. Not many, but enough to get by on. And she loved to sing as a kid, but she never thought it would end up being her profession. She had planned on being a teacher. She was always off reading somewhere. They had a good amount of land, a good number of trees for her to read beneath. Can you see her there?" she asked. "Can you see her as a thin, small thing off reading somewhere? Not confident yet. Not shapely. Just small, a small, distant thing."

"I can see it," said Tanner.

They each took a sip. The light was still bright at their table. Some country song and Hope's voice rose above the din of the other patrons' chatter.

"But how did she end up here?" he said.

Courtney looked over at Hope, and then back at Tanner. "She got pregnant young," Courtney said. "But not too young. At some point in her early twenties. And she was off at college. Away from here. Some place not as green. And she decided that she needed to come back here. She told her boyfriend about it. About the pregnancy. And she described her hometown to him. He was from the city, and he'd never owned a lawnmower before. And she told him how quickly the grass would grow there, and that he would need to get a lawnmower if he wanted to come with them. That she would like it if he would come with them. But she told him that that was it. That that was the option. She was going to go home. She couldn't imagine raising a child anywhere else. A child needs grass to play on, she told him. A child needs grass, not a concrete courtyard shared by the whole apartment complex."

Tanner had been holding on to his glass while Courtney spoke. He brought it forward then, and then he finished off the rest of it. "And the singing?" he said.

"Extra money," she said. "She teaches during the day. She did become a teacher after all. And she sings here two nights a week. She says it's for the extra money, but they could get by without it. She does it because she likes to feel confident. Look at her. She's beautiful. The men fall in love with her. These men here. Look. They are falling in love with her now."

"And the women?"

"They love her too."

"Because they want to be her."

"No," she said. "I don't think so. I think . . . I think it's because they are her."

"You're getting drunk," he said.

"No, I'm not," she said. "Look. A glass and a half. And I don't want this now. I'm done. Finish this one. Here. Finish this one for me."

He took the glass and set it on his side of the table. Hope was walking in their direction. She had been visiting with other tables but had not yet stopped by theirs. She was walking toward them, singing, her breath pausing at the end of each verse while her steps carried her forward steadily. She looked at Courtney as she neared the table, and Courtney looked back at her, putting on a heavy expression to let her know that she would prefer it if she didn't stop there, the same expression Courtney would give her teachers as a child when she wished to let them know that she didn't want to be called on. Courtney gave her that look, her lips pressed together, the line formed by their connection caving inward slightly, and Hope kept walking by, but as she did, Courtney reached out for her hand, saying to her as her fingers brushed the back of her free hand, "You are lovely."

story at midnight

So I'm filling up at the Arco station on Seventh Street. It's about midnight on Tuesday. I stopped shooting pool early because I have that Geography GE on Monday Wednesday Friday. So I'm filling up because I hate getting gas in the mornings, and I'm about halfway through filling the tank when these two women come up and ask me for a ride.

I say, No. Sorry.

Then the older one, probably in her forties, maybe early fifties, real seasoned looking but you could tell she was really pretty once. I mean, she was good looking now, but definitely, she'd seen some days. Her hair and clothes weren't completely messy or anything. I mean she wasn't disheveled, but she wasn't fresh looking either. So this older one says that they have money to pay for gas. But she pulls out this ziplock bag full of change. I mean the bag was full. It was all weighed down with coins, sagging in her hand. And she said the cabs won't take it.

But I still said, Sorry. Good luck to you. And I smiled at her. And I kept pumping the gas.

And the younger girl I couldn't really see at this point. She was standing a few feet behind the seasoned gal, and she was on her cell phone. And then the older one walked away, and the younger one followed. And I saw them walk up to this slick looking dude in this dropped Civic or some such terrible car, and it's funny because I got this real uneasy feeling. I didn't want these two girls to drive off with that dude. But I could tell he said no, and he wasn't as cordial as I was. Plus my tank was all full, and I put the pump back and twisted on the gas cap.

So they walk up to me again, and this time, the younger one is right next to the seasoned one, and she's off her phone, and the older one talks but the younger is also looking right at me. And the older one is asking for a ride again, saying again that they've got that bag of gas money, and I'm looking at her, and I'm looking at the younger one, who also has kind of light brown hair to her shoulders, but her nose is a little more pointed, and her skin doesn't have any wrinkles yet, and she's pretty too but I think the older one would have been prettier if they were the same age, but definitely this younger one is hovering around twenty, definitely not above twenty-five, and I'm standing there about to get in my car, about to drive home, about to sleep or do some homework, and I know these girls will keep asking people until they get a ride from someone. And I'm starting to worry about them because who knows whose car they'd end up in, right?

So I say, Sure. I'll take you guys.

And the seasoned one says, Thanks so much. You're real sweet.

And the younger one doesn't say anything.

And then they each open a backseat door and climb in. And I'm thinking, Wow, these girls are trusting. I guess I look like a pretty decent guy. And I'm thinking that they're lucky that I'm a pretty decent guy after all.

So I get in too, and I start up the car, and then I feel like a chauffeur, and I was wishing that one of them had sat up in the front, but then again they don't know I'm a nice guy, so it was probably smart to at least stay in the backseat together if you're going to accept a ride from a stranger.

The seasoned one tells me to take a left on Seventh, and I do, and then the whole drive only took about five minutes. And I had Minor Threat playing because that was what was in the tape player. And the seasoned one said that she used to listen to them when she was younger. She said that the tape was taking her back. It was nostalgic for her. And I don't remember what songs were on for the drive, but I'm sitting there with them behind me, and I'm looking in the rearview as often as I can. Not to check them out or anything, but just to kind of get a sense of them. You know. I just wanted to be let in on their lives, and all of a sudden I was really wanting us to have some serious conversation about something, or I wanted them to ask me about me so they could get to know me. But we didn't talk much. And I didn't think to ask them questions about themselves.

So there isn't much conversation after the first few minutes talking about music, and I keep driving where the older one directs me. And before too long we arrive at a motel. And I've seen this one before in the day time. And I've never liked the look of it. And I pull my car to the curb where she tells me to. And the young one is out of the backseat the second the wheels stop. But the seasoned one leans forward and tells me, Thank you, and she holds out that ziplock back, and with the back door still open the overhead light is on, and I can really see the bag clearly for the first time. And it's a mess of pennies, nickels, dimes, and maybe a few quarters, but the dirty copper pennies stand out the most. Sad looking compared to the shiny silver here and there in the bag.

I say, No thanks. You keep that. This ride's on me.

Then she says, You're a darling. We need more of them like you. And she scoots over to the curbside backdoor still open. And she gets out and shuts it, and the light in the car goes out, all symbolic like, and that was the last I saw of them. And I didn't pull away at first. I looked for them to see if they'd be okay. But after the door shut, they were just gone, so they must have walked toward the trunk instead of the engine.

But I wish I saw them enter a room together with no one else. I wish I saw them walk up to a door, pull out their key, and then go safely in. But I don't know what happened to them—friend and friend, mother and daughter, teacher and protégé—who knows. I wish I'd said, Hey, I've got this full tank of gas. Let's drive somewhere. Let's drive up the coast as far as a tank of gas will take us. Let's drive until some patch of light lets us know the night is almost over, and then let's pull aside and find a diner, and let's dump those coins on our table and count them up, ordering three coffees and maybe some eggs and toast if there's enough.

in a laundromat in long beach

Sidestepping in, back pressed against the glass door, he's caught off guard by all the women and their children. He's caught off guard, he realizes, because there were so few cars in the lot outside, where seconds ago he parked their Corolla and then managed to pull free the large storage bin wedged into the backseat. Halfway in the Laundromat, he holds the blue plastic storage bin he's using as a hamper. It's full of new clothes he bought yesterday from a saleswoman at Nordstrom Rack way over in Laguna Hills. He lets the door slide off his back. Fully inside now, his eyes adjust to the brightness of the overhead lights, and he remembers that this is how Laundromats are, all bright and spacious, rows of machines buzzing and rows of connected chairs, mostly orange, filled with people biding their time, and it occurs to him, because of that brightness, that it was gray outside, even dull outside, and that he is pleased to be here. He finds two empty washing machines in one of the outer rows and sets down his storage bin of clothes.

She'd wanted to keep the minivan, and he agreed that would be best, but he'd found himself missing it already this morning. After he'd gone back to the house and dumped the Christmas ornaments on their garage floor and after he'd tossed his new clothes into the Christmas storage bin, having already removed the tags and those long thin stickers some of them had, he couldn't quite maneuver his new hamper into the Corolla's trunk, so he was forced to cram it into the backseat and drive to the Laundromat with his own seat uncomfortably pushed forward.

At the washing machines, he tosses in unworn clothes. First the Brioni shirt that Caroline had discovered hidden among the cheaper Ralph Laurens, and then other shirts, and then the pants, more pants than he'd remembered getting. Caroline, that's the Laguna Hills saleswoman who so expertly assisted him, pulling him through the racks—No, no, she'd said. Not pleats. You're done with those. Okay? No more pleated pants for you—and he wasn't quite sure what she'd meant, but he said, Okay, and then he let her stack non-pleated pants on his arm, and she regularly slid her free fingers across the back of the hand she pulled, causing him to shiver each time and each time extracting a small amount of his courage so that he had nothing left in him to ask her on a date after she had finished helping him and escorted him to the check-out line.

He pushes down the pants around the second washer's cylinder, making room for the boxer briefs. They're the last items in the storage-bin-turned-hamper, clumped together in a little mound. Twelve of them, six to a pack, each with a unique color or pattern. He grabs the pair on top, a deep maroon pair with thin black stripes. Forgetting where he is, he presses the pair against himself, flat against his front, holding them tightly in place, stretching the waistband across his belt at each end with each thumb and pointing finger pinched together at his sides. He'd done the same thing last night in his Extended Stay America mini suite, standing in front of the full-length mirror in Night One of the free week stay he'd racked up from company-paid trips. He figured a week would be long enough to find his own apartment, and if not, he could always spring for the second week himself. He held up the navy blue pair last night, the ones with the little white dots, and in his curiosity he stripped down, removing his familiar clothes. Especially familiar were the loose boxer shorts, and after he stripped down, he put on the boxer briefs, and they were tight, tight everywhere, even at the fabric around his thighs, and he stared at himself, and he recognized himself, of course, and he was familiar with the shape of his body even in the unfamiliar room with the unfamiliar objects—lamp, bed, desk—that were behind him but reflected next to him, and he was familiar with that small arc of flesh that hung over the waistbands of his boxers and that now hung over those tight blue boxer briefs, and he thought to himself, or did he even whisper it—I don't know if this feels different—and he knew that the tightness was different, certainly, that his body was being cupped by the briefs, his skin being pressed as it had not since he stopped wearing tight underwear during his sophomore year of high school thirty years ago, but he still could not decide if he felt different otherwise, and he stood there, and the fabric gripping his thighs caused his thighs to pulse and his skin to itch, especially the small spaces of skin around his hair follicles, and the pulsing and itching made him want to scream, but he did not know what to scream, so he remained in statuesque torment and ultimately decided that the itchiness was caused by the rigidity of the unwashed fabric and that he'd better get to a Laundromat at some point tomorrow. And now he is pressing against himself the maroon pair with the black stripes, and he is being looked at by the two women closest to him, and he realizes now that they have been watching him, and he throws into the washer the maroon briefs and then all the others until the storage bin is empty.

He walks to the end of the row of washers where a vending machine stands against the wall. The bigger kids are playing video games. There's an old Pac-Man and some kind of military game. He examines the little boxes of detergents behind the glass. They look odd to him held in the air like that, suspended in rows and columns by those spirals he's used to seeing candy bars and chips trapped in. He chooses the little box with the color image of mountains and grass and flowers. At his washers, he dumps in some of the powder. But seeing it clump, he then eases up on the box's angle and flicks his wrist to spread the remaining white particles more freely on the other tops of the exposed boxer briefs, imagining that this somewhat carefree yet somewhat calculated dispersal is the same technique used in sowing wildflower seeds, producing the same balanced unevenness shown in the little color blotches dotting the green grass on the lower half of the now-empty detergent box he is holding. He inserts his quarters into the two machines, turns each dial to hold/cold, and shuts the lids once he sees the water spilling out onto his two piles of new clothes, saturating the layers of briefs, pants, and shirts crammed together into clumps of newness. He almost splurged for socks and undershirts too but decided to cut back spending where it wasn't necessary. Even today he is wearing an old pair of socks and an old undershirt, along with his last pair of loose-fitting boxer shorts, having stuffed the rest of his boxers and all of his old collared shirts and pants—did they all have pleats, he wonders—into a Salvation Army collection bin on Seventh Street.

With his washers washing, he sits down in one of the orange chairs. The chair's vivid orange makes him aware of the new polo shirt and pants combination he is wearing, lime-green up top and blue-gray below, a combo Caroline said would make him look more youthful but that he is now afraid might seem ridiculous against the orange backdrop. The pants itch him. He crosses his legs and remembers that there is waiting involved in doing laundry, and he is upset with himself for not grabbing a book, but he does not have any books in his Extended Stay America mini suite anyway, and then he thinks about his books at his home—his old home—and wonders if there are any worth keeping, but there aren't really, and now he wishes he remembered to grab the complimentary hotel paper at least.

A few of the smaller kids run about through the rows of washers, stooping to hide from one another as they scurry along, shaping their hands into guns ready to be fired at whoever might discover them. Their movements bring about the attention of their mothers, who every so often lift their eyes from the folding tables or machines in front of them, take inventory with some glances around the room, and then return to their tasks. He sits and waits, and a portly woman in a yellow floral sundress walks in his direction from the dryers, and he expects her to turn as she gets closer to him, but instead she comes right up to him and gracefully plops down beside him, her left leg touching his right, and he is surprised and confused, but she shifts her body to sort of half face him, and she says to him as if they are old acquaintances, "It's my older son. He's the problem."

And he says, "Pardon?"

And the portly woman says, "My older son. Do you want to know what he did this morning?"

And he says, "Okay."

And the portly woman says, "Well," but then she pauses, and then she asks, "What's your name?"

And he says, "Gerry."

"Well, Gerry," she goes on, "I came into the boys' room to gather up their clothes for washing, and I saw that Isaac was playing one of his games."

She pauses again, and he feels as though he is supposed to contribute something, so he asks, "What kind of game?"

"A video game," she says. "I spoiled the boys by putting my old TV in there. So Isaac is playing his game while the little one is sleeping. That's him right there." She points to where two small boys are sitting on top of a washer, kicking its side with their heels. "The one on the right," she says," and then in a louder voice, "Not too hard, sweetie."

The boy's cheeks ripen with embarrassment at *sweeetie*.

"Sure enough," she continues, tapping a finger on the man's leg to recapture his focus, "Sure enough, as I was gathering the clothes, I noticed I didn't recognize the game he was playing."

There's another pause, and again he's feeling as though he's supposed to contribute something here, so he asks, "And what's the problem?"

"The problem," she says, "is that I bought that game player with two games. One has race cars, and the other is a rodent that eats things. This was one of those fighting games."

"And you don't want him playing fighting games."

"Not really, come to think of it. But that wasn't the problem." She looks back over at her younger son, who sits by himself now, legs dangling calmly against a still machine, an aimless look on his face. "The problem is I didn't buy it for him."

And there's another pause when he senses her expectation for him to say something. But he feels as though he's missing out on the point, or the problem still, so he remains quiet.

"He stole it," she says.

And he sees how she could jump to that conclusion, but he says, "I'm sure he just bought it for himself."

"Not with the five dollars a week I give him."

"But if he saved it up."

"He doesn't save it."

"Well, he could have borrowed the game from a friend."

"His friends don't share things," she says, "not valuable things anyway." There are fewer people in the large bright room now. There are fewer machines buzzing. "He's fourteen," she says, "fourteen years old." Her voice is heavy, and for the first time he feels as though he has been let in on some intimate thing, this woman's problem, and he wonders what he looked like from across the room when she decided that he was someone worth confiding in, when she must have thought to herself—There, over there, that's the person here I want to talk to—or was it that he was the only unoccupied, unconversing adult in the room at the moment she walked over to him?—he doesn't know—and is this what people do in Laundromats?—find strangers to talk to—and if you're alone, can you not be alone?—does current Laundromat etiquette require conversation with neighbors?—and was it only yesterday when he drove down to Laguna Hills to shop for his new life and saw the saleswoman who would introduce herself as *Caroline, here to assist*, and didn't he see her before she saw him, and didn't he position himself near the racks where Caroline would find him after he had seen her, and didn't he want to smell her young hair when he saw her meandering through the racks of clothes, and didn't he hope that he would graze her often as they walked together collecting things of her choosing? And the woman in the floral sundress beside him now is not interested in the smell of his hair, he knows this, and she is interested only in the well-being of her sons, and she is talking to him about this, and he is not special; he is just there, sitting, being available, and she pounced on his availability, and she has just said heavily, "fourteen years old."

And he says, "He'll turn out all right. Fourteen is still young enough to do stupid things."

And she says, "Thanks, hon. Thanks, Gerry," and squeezes his knee, then brings her hands to her belly and arches backward. "But he'll be upset for a while. I'm afraid of not seeing him for a day or two."

"What did you do?" he says.

"When I saw I didn't recognize his game, I took it out of the machine and asked him where he got it. His eyes were searching around like they were going to say something for him, and before he could make up some lie, I broke it, smashed it with my foot."

Gerry nods slowly, not approving or disapproving but soaking in the decision, expecting to be asked what he would have done if he and one of his own children were in that situation.

"There was nothing else to be done," she says. "I wasn't about to march him back to the store and pay for it myself. And I can't risk turning him in. They don't give kids hand slaps like they did for us. And I couldn't very well let him keep it. There was nothing else to be done."

"So how did he take it?" says Gerry.

"Like a boy who wants his way. He gripped this or that, then slammed the door and left the house. And I saw him walking down the street while I stood at his window. He was cool as a cucumber. He's too big for me to chase after him and drag him home. So I just let him stroll on by while I burned my eyes into his cheek. Then I remembered why I'd gone in there in the first place and started picking up their clothes."

"And now you're here."

"And now I'm here."

A few seconds pass and she says that she can see that her clothes have stopped tumbling. She wishes him a good day and walks back over to the dryers, pulling out her boys' clothes and piling them in a cart, wheeling them down to an empty table where she starts her folding.

He gets up too and checks on his clothes in the two washers. They're done, and he lifts the lids to find the wet clothes clinging to the cylinders in the center of each machine. He smiles at the smallness of freshly washed clothes. It has been a long time since he has seen this marvel, the clunkiness of clothes dismantled or simplified or, he supposes, just made comprehensible somehow, this clean dampness that must be short-lived before it becomes harmful. Maybe he has been apathetic. Or maybe that's still not the right word. But that's what his wife said a couple of days ago before she drove away in the minivan with their son and daughter so he could be alone in the house to gather his things.

He pulls out the wet clothes and piles them into a loose laundry cart. The portly woman in the floral sundress is nearing the end of her folding. Her little son walks up to her and tugs on her dress, and she picks him up and sets him on the table. His feet hang high above the floor, and then he pulls in his legs and hugs them, and he lets his eyes close as his forehead rests against his knees. The door to the Laundromat opens and a young man walks in and heads straight toward the round woman and little boy. He stands beside her and helps fold the last few articles. Neither of them speaks. They fold mechanically and silently until the job is done, and then the older son stacks and lifts their two hampers and nudges awake his little brother with an elbow.

These three are walking toward the door, mother and sons, and Gerry's hand is on the cold metal of his laundry cart, and he cannot let them leave, but they are leaving, and he shouts, "Wait!" and they and the few people remaining all turn to face him, and he runs toward the trio, pulling the cart of sopping new clothes behind him, and he says to the older son whose stolen video game was broken that morning, "Take these clothes. I don't want them. You can have them. You'll need them soon. You're getting older. Take them. Look, they're nice. They're good ones. I've never worn them. But you have to dry them. Make sure to dry them so they don't get ruined. Do it now if you can. Here are quarters," and Gerry reaches into his pocket and retrieves his quarters for the dryer, and he sets them on a table by the young man, and the young man says, "Thanks," and the woman in the sundress is quiet, her forehead perplexed, but now it is Gerry's turn to tell a story, so he says, "Yesterday I wanted these clothes, but I don't want them now. And I don't want these either," and Gerry takes off his lime-green polo shirt and his blue-gray pants, pushing off his new lace-less shoes too in the process, and he sets the shirt and pants and shoes on top of the wet clothes, and he says, "These are new too. I only wore them today. Take them, okay," and Gerry is standing there in his old socks, and his old boxer shorts, and his old undershirt, and the room is quiet, and the room is bright and is always bright when the rows of fluorescent lights gleam on the ceiling, and Gerry runs for the door in his socks and boxers, but then he remembers the empty Christmas ornament bin he'd used as a hamper that day, and he runs back to the other side of the room and picks up the empty plastic bin, his socks slipping beneath him as he searches for traction, and with the ornament bin gripped to his chest, he darts for the door and leaves the bright room behind, racing down the street as fast as his middle-aged frame can carry him, and his body is churning inside, his blood knocking along its pathways, and his moving skin is already a hot wet, and the bin grows heavy in his arms even though it is empty, and he runs forward, and he is not thinking about his keys or wallet in his abandoned pants, and he is not wondering if he'll be able to get his old clothes back from the thrift store, and he is not thinking of the miles he'll have to run in socks with new holes growing or of the thickening grayness or of the cars passing him and the people staring at a spectacle they do not understand, trying to figure out, with their side view, what this madman is carrying so frantically.

ascending and descending in macarthur

T hom drove his rental car out of the Oakland airport and headed to his old neighborhood, his plane having landed at 10:30 on a clear East Bay Sunday morning, away from San Francisco's peninsular fog. He sped down Hegenberger Road with the windows open, the cool air enlivening his skin as it shook off the last of the stuffiness from his packed flight from Philadelphia. After months of trying, his wife Julie had convinced him that they should attend his twenty-year high school reunion. Her plane would land in a couple hours, also from Philadelphia but with a stop in Denver, so he had a bit of time to use up before driving back to the airport to get her. Since becoming parents, both Thom and Julie agreed that if they ever needed to fly somewhere without their daughter, they would take separate flights. This, they reasoned, practically ensured that one of them would make it back alive to their child. What would their sweet infant Eva do if both of her parents died tragically in some plane crash, they'd worried, and now that Eva was eight and at home with Julie's parents staying with her for the week, they still felt better taking different flights.

Hegenberger Road merged into 73rd Avenue, and the cool morning air still felt great on his skin and in his hair, and he kept his windows down as he slowed to a stoplight even though this was East Oakland, and when the light turned green he accelerated quickly but did not speed, and when he got to MacArthur Boulevard, he hung a left and headed into the safer part of East Oakland where he grew up, and as he travelled down MacArthur familiar things popped out at him. More and more. Familiar things that twenty years

20

can change but not undo. Familiar things that didn't make him happy or sad but that filled him with that sense of wonderment one gets from stumbling upon an object misplaced so long ago it stopped being acknowledged as missing. He slowed the car to absorb these marvels. The flat architecture of the mostly one-story buildings, the mature trees, the fading red letters of the video store sign—REGAL VIDEO—which seemed to have stayed in business somehow. And then there were the dozens of churches and liquor stores lining the boulevard, about one of each per block, most of them single-shop storefronts with a rectangular sign above the door. Two blocks ago there was JESUS IS THE ANSWER COMMUNITY CHURCH, and just to Thom's right was LARRY'S LAND OF LIQUOR. And when he moved away for college Thom had learned that Philadelphia's inner city neighborhoods were also dotted with churches and liquor stores, and even though he knew that everyone could guess the reasons why, he still felt clever when at eighteen and on one of their lengthy freshmen walking dates he'd turned to Julie and said, "The streets are filled with churches and liquor stores in places where people need hope and escape. Those two things," he'd said, "hope and escape, are closely related. It's that way back home." And Julie was from an affluent Philadelphia suburb, and Thom's young self-imagined that she felt safe there huddled beside him while they walked to nowhere in particular so that they could be together outside of their dorm rooms.

Thom turned the car off the main road and into his old residential neighborhood. He drove mechanically, slowing at stop signs, curving at curves. The landscape shifted the way it always had, offering a curious mixture of dilapidated houses and well-kept homes along each street. Now approaching one corner of his old street, he pulled the rental car to the curb beside a bright blue mailbox, his childhood mailbox, which had always been a faded blue that his mother complained about, but now here it was, freshly painted only after his parents had followed him back east a decade ago when in his twenties he'd said he was staying there but invited them to live nearby, and the news of his staying and his invitation for them to travel east were accompanied by the news of Julie's pregnancy, and it was a joyous moment in what had been a sad stack of years for Thom and his parents, and now here in his old neighborhood Thom stopped the car, and he got out of the car, and he approached his childhood mailbox, and he opened the metal mouth and looked inside, and he thought about the times his mother asked him and

21

his brother Evan to carry the piles of Christmas cards down the street to the mailbox, and they were such good sons together, opening the mouth of the faded blue mailbox, where they would pour in the dozens of angel-stamped envelopes containing his mother's yearly Christmas letter—*The Dilsby Times*, she'd titled it, giving each year a new volume number. Bored one day as kids, the boys read through the early letters their mom kept in a binder on a bookshelf in the family room. Volume 1 recalled the first four months with little Thomas, bragging about how good he was at "tummy time," how he was a pro at holding his head up and rolling over, how they expected him to crawl any day now. Volume 2 showcased Thomas's incredible walking and word abilities. And Volume 3 disclosed what a good big brother toddler Thomas had been once little Evan joined the family in the spring, and then it bragged equally about Evan's "tummy time" achievements. And so went *The Dilsby Times* for twenty years, reporting on science experiments and track meets, offering photo coverage of the boys off to church camp in the summer, off to a school dance in spring, then winter, the lucky girls beside the strapping boys, corsages on wrists, pastel petals in the spring shot, red and white in the winter one. And now touching the newly painted mailbox, feeling the cold metal that should be a faded blue, he knew he didn't want to see his childhood home anymore. His parents living back east near him now—his brother having passed away eighteen years ago, a month before his high school graduation, when he'd just turned eighteen and Thom was twenty—he now had only an opaque sense of the old house—its structure, two narrow stories—its layout, the boys' bedrooms upstairs with the second bathroom—its detached garage to house one-day-needed things. And touching the newly painted mailbox, fingertips, then palm, he knew now he was wrong to want to see the old house and that whatever reaction he would have to taking in its chipping paint or its fresh paint or its whatever paint would be a reaction he could do without, and so he got back in the rental car, drove away from his old street, and headed down MacArthur toward his childhood movie theater to kill some time before returning to the airport to pick up Julie.

While he drove the few blocks to the theater, his left ear itched and he scratched it. Sometimes he would resist scratching for a minute or two—to show some of the resolve that Dr. Müller had, his high school Art History teacher and proponent for resisting itches when something more pressing was at hand—but he scratched right away this time and relished the quick relief, skating a fingernail over his lobe, back and forth, back and forth, until the tingling stopped and his hand returned to the wheel and his lobe was left only with the memory of his own touch. He pushed the gas pedal down more, and the outside air rushed through the windows and through his hair and across so much of his skin—his face and neck, his ears and lips—and over his left arm, exposed where his shirt sleeve had been rolled up, his thick arm hairs bullied by the wind, forced back like wheat stalks on a flat prairie. And the wind racing over him felt good, but his ear itched again, and then his scalp in multiple places, and his arm as well, and after he stopped at the curb in front of the movie theater, he pulled both hands off the wheel and scratched with frantic fingers, and new itches surfaced as others were quelled, and he thought his skin must be more irritable today from being in the stuffed-up plane for so long.

He turned off the car and checked his watch. It was a quarter till noon. He didn't care what was playing. He just hoped the earliest movie hadn't started yet because he hated missing the beginnings of things. The box building wasn't too promising; its sign, MACARTHUR THEATER, had been removed from its large flat front, but the words remained legible because of the discolored paint, the sign's letters having blocked the sun for so many years before being torn away from the stucco. He approached the theater's large glass doors. It was dark behind them, and he assumed the place had been shut down, but he reached out for the brass handle anyway, and when he pulled, the door swung open freely, and he stepped onto the maroon carpet with black floral patterns, unchanged in decades, and as he walked further into the lobby he could see in the dimness a woman standing in front of the ticket booth. This was where he and Evan would often pass their time as kids, especially in the summer. This was where he and Evan relished in hearing grown men up on the screen swear strange and vibrant words. This was where he and Evan caught their first glimpses of unclothed breasts, watching R-rated movies instead of the PG ones they'd told their parents they were off to see. The woman in front of the ticket booth started walking toward him. She looked slightly older than he was, perhaps in her early forties. She walked with slow determination, nothing hesitant in her steps. And now a few feet away. Black slip-on shoes. Good firm ankles. Tan skirt below the knees. Dark blue sweater. Brown hair in a bun. Thin pleasant lips. Thin pleasant smile revealing two crooked lower teeth, also pleasant, leaning into each other. And she extended her hand and said, "Welcome. It's in there," pointing to the inside doors leading to the old theater.

And Thom grabbed her hand and then released its warmth back to her, and, confused, he said, "Thank you. It's in there?" pointing to the same doors.

"Yes," she said. "Enjoy." And she left him to go back to her post in front of the ticket counter.

"Thank you," Thom said again. And he walked to the theater doors and pushed them open and went inside.

Inside, the movie theater carpet had been torn out, but the rows of seats were all there, and they were filled with people sitting and watching a man where the screen should have been, a man up on a stage, and he was large and round and was holding a microphone and a book that must have been a Bible, and Thom knew then, of course, that he had entered a church service and that the old theater had indeed closed down, and he paused there in the aisle toward the back, standing on cement that had been painted maroon, a maroon like a cabernet or, better yet, the grape juice in those tiny plastic communion cups he would drink whenever they happened to make it to their own church on the first Sunday of the month. The floor was that communion cup red, and it wasn't just the color but the lights reflecting on the paint, the semi-bright overhead lighting that must have been installed after the theater became a church, the lights that cast little bright spots on the cement floor, and for these long seconds Thom still stared at the maroon floor and the spots of light ahead of his feet, and he was still thinking of communion cups because in the times he held each little plastic cup back home, his index finger and thumb encircling the cool plastic, the flat nickel-size opening would always have a dot of light in the center, and before he would take the cup and drink he would try to think the right things and he would consider what it meant that there was a bit of light reflected in the maroon, and he would angle the cup here and there and the light would move around, and he would pray for his wife and his daughter and his brother, and he would sometimes think about transubstantiation, and he wondered if that ever happened, and he wondered if people still tasted wine if that happened, and he didn't know many Catholics, and he only ever thought about asking when he was in his own protestant pew about to drink grape juice, so he would probably never ask anyone, and he thought that symbols were strong enough things, and he thought that this floor was its own sign as he stood like a hesitant boy on unfamiliar ice.

Thom looked up from the floor and took a seat toward the back.

The preacher was somewhere in his sermon. "Do you hear what I'm saying to you, belovéd? The father of the sick son said, 'Sure, I believe. But I need you to help my unbelief!' And that's what I'm going to talk to you about this morning. Faith and doubt." The preacher paused. Clearly he was just getting started. Thom settled in his back seat, fascinated by everything—the old theater turned church, the good-sized crowd inside despite the lack of signage outside, the imposing figure down below, his raspy, seasoned voice. "Faith and doubt," the preacher went on. "Have you ever said that in so many words?—I believe but help my unbelief. Have you ever said that?"

"Indeed!" said a woman near the front.

"And in our world," said the preacher, "in a world like ours, how can we live in faith? And once we're in faith, do we ever doubt again? And is it okay to doubt? I want to tell you all something. And listen closely. I want to tell you all that doubt is okay. I believe in doubt! Did you hear what I just said? I believe in doubt! But what words do I have this morning for those who suffer with doubt? For those who wrestle with doubt? Doubt is a real deal struggle for many. It was for me, and I bet it is for many of you sitting here today. We question whether there can be a good God in a world where so many bad things happen. In a world where innocent kids are shot by mistake. In a world where so many addictions tear apart our families. In a world where people are hungry and neglected. And I'm not just talking about off in other countries. But right here. Right here in our city, our neighbors are suffering. And so we wonder, how can a good God exist in all of this grime and selfishness, in this despair and hardship? And there are people who turn to the word of God, who open the Bible, and they have questions, and they read, and they pray, and they cry out, and they don't find relief. And maybe they believe a little bit, but there just isn't enough of a response to push them over the edge into belief."

The preacher paused and began nodding his head. He stood in the middle of the stage, microphone in one hand, Bible in the other, no podium, no notes. And he nodded while looking around the theater turned sanctuary. "There's a lot to say," he went on, "and I can't say it all in a single sermon, but the first point I need you to hear is that doubting is a good place to be. If you are doubting, you are thinking, you are probing, you are in a wilderness, and you know you're not happy there, not satisfied there, and the wilderness of doubt has pathways that lead in different directions, and one of those is faith. Doubt can lead you to faith. And doubt is not a weakness. Doubt is not a sin. Belovéd, don't you let anybody tell you doubt is a sin." The preacher paused again and seemed to be locating his next bullet point. After a moment, he said, "I want to tell you a story about curiosity. We all know that curiosity can be a dangerous thing. But here is an example of good curiosity."

One of the last paintings Thom remembered studying in Dr. Müller's Art History course was Penck's *The Demon of Curiosity*. He thought about it sometimes, perhaps once or twice a year, maybe more, because it was one of the paintings discussed on the day of the "itch tangent," as he and his classmates had called it before graduating and seeing less and less of each other. It was during Thom's last week of high school. He and his classmates had already taken the advanced placement exam, but Dr. Müller insisted that the students still meet for class. The room was warm with the anticipation of summer. Dr. Müller was a slight man, both short and thin. He wore a suit, or at the very least a sports coat and dress pants, and he always had a tie on and seldom removed his jacket. Instead of typical dress shoes, he wore dress boots with three-inch heels. But even in his boots, he was noticeably short, and in an effort to combat whatever hindrance his shortness caused him as a lecturer, his desk had been raised up a few feet off the ground, placed at an angle in the corner of the room on top of a custom built wooden platform. While sitting at his desk, Dr. Müller could peer over the students and also look at the screen where he would project images of whatever paintings, sculptures, and buildings they were studying. On the day of the itch tangent, a projection of Penck's painting filled the pull-down screen at the front of the class. The room was dim, and Dr. Müller held the long-corded remote for his slide projector, standing on the platform, in front of his desk. They had just discussed Salle's *Miner*, and Dr. Müller had said something about post-modern painting really being late modern painting because of the traditional shackles of canvas, paint, and brushes, and Dr. Müller had asked the class about the man's pregnant belly in *The Demon of Curiosity*, and when no one generated an answer fast enough, he climbed down the steps of his dais in his red-brown boots and a grey three-piece suit, and then he grabbed his long wooden pointing stick and rapped the middle of the image at the red man's swelled stomach. "You said he was full of signs, did you not?" The man in the painting was indeed full of letters and numbers and signs, and that much the students pointed out to him quickly. And they agreed too that he was full of knowledge and that the two-headed bird perched on the demon to the left of the red man symbolized curiosity since each head looked in a different direction. And Dr. Müller stood before the image waiting for someone to tackle the man's pregnancy, beads of sweat on his forehead glistening in the projector's light, a majority of the students clearly having checked out for the summer already.

With only a few days of school remaining, the seniors especially had grown bold in various aspects of their institutional life. Thom was less concerned with the tidiness of his uniform. His tie could be loosened a bit at the neck, the top button even left unbuttoned. No amount of late-year uniform violations would take away his almost full scholarship to Temple. And some students had become bolder in how they addressed their teachers, but Thom thought that was taking things too far.

Unanswered, Dr. Müller stood there in the light of Penck's painting, or in the light filtered through the slide containing a translucent image of Penck's painting, and Thom took note of the sweat on his forehead and the tightness of his tie's knot, a Full Windsor no less, and the glistening buttons of his vest and the apparent heaviness of his jacket, all in the near-summer heat, so Thom had asked in concern, as well as in curiosity, "Dr. Müller, why don't you take off your jacket?"

Dr. Müller faced Thom, and Thom regretted his question because he did not want to upset someone he admired so much, but Dr. Müller's expression shifted from an unsignifying blankness to a familiar half-smile with closed lips, and Thom relaxed at the understandable image, and then he leaned forward in his front-row seat because he knew that a slow response from him was always a thoughtful response, and Thom felt at his back and sides the weight of the class behind him and beside him leaning forward toward the small figure who always—yes, always—said something of importance no matter the topic. Dr. Müller widened his glance to include the whole room, and his eyes shifted about from face to face, and then he replied to Thom's question and said, "I would never do that."

Dr. Müller gave up no more than that, but the students knew that it would take only another prod or two to reveal more, so someone else behind Thom chipped in and asked, "But aren't you hot, Dr. Müller?"

"Of course I am," he said. "But that is no reason to remove my coat. For what would be next? The loosening of my tie? The unbuttoning of my collar?" He paused and made a point to look around at the late-teenage boys in the class. Thom tightened up his tie when Dr. Müller moved his stare from him to one of the other boys. "I think not," he went on. "I will stay as I am dressed until I reach the comfort of my home. That is where one should feel comfortable. Not the classroom." He paused again, and none of the students dared say anything because they all knew he was just getting started on something. "This problem of comfort extends beyond the classroom. Consider this. If I am in our chapel service, or if I am discussing some matter with a colleague, or with a student, and an itch develops in my ear or on my forehead, I will not scratch it." His eyes widened. "I will not scratch it," he said again. "I will sing the hymn, I will contemplate the homily, I will consider the words of whoever is speaking to me, but I will not raise my hand to my face to relieve myself of the itch. When I am no longer occupied by something more important, if the itch has not retreated, then I will scratch it. I will scratch it only then. Only when I am ready to let it have my attention. And now you ask me, 'Are you not hot? Why do you not remove your jacket?' And you are a smart bunch. You know that I am hot. We are all hot together. But I am not bothered by this heat. For me, the heat is of far less interest than this slide of Penck. You might be thinking that this is a discipline. You might be misunderstanding this as self-control. No. This is more than a mindset. This is an art." He nodded, and his forehead wrinkled, and he seemed to be working this idea out for himself, and then he said again, "This is an art." And Dr. Müller paused, and the students waited to hear if he was done, and he looked at Thom, who now sat up straight with his top button buttoned and his tie tightened, and he said, "Thomas, I thank you for your concern." And he removed from his suit jacket one of his handkerchiefs with a cursive *M* stitched on it, and he wiped sweat from his forehead, and then he folded the handkerchief neatly and put it back in his jacket pocket, and he said, "I thank you, Thomas, but I will remove my jacket when I am home. For now, will someone please tell me about the red man's swelling? If he is full of knowledge and if he is about to give birth to something, then who else aided in conception? And why is his mouth upward, and why is he pointing to his head with one hand and his belly with the other? Or is he scratching his head and his belly?"

In the old theater seat, in the room that was now a church, Thom's head itched and he scratched it. But he regretted it because he was in one of those situations that Dr. Müller said required self-regulation. Focus on the sermon, he might say to him now in his Austrian-Hungarian accent, thinned hair neat and tidy. Scratch the itch when there is nothing more pressing for your mind to attend to, he might say. But as it often is with itches, Thom's head itched again, and this time he didn't scratch it, and this time he focused on the preacher's words—"Someone once said: Many people think that God is fragile and needs to be protected from questions, needs to be shielded from some grand question that will undo him, some question that would make faith for the rest of us impossible. Many people think that questions have the power to smash God, as if God is a clay pot as if God can be broken apart and made unrecognizable or unfixable because of the power of tough questions. No! He's not fragile. Our God's not fragile. Don't make the mistake of thinking that the tough questions that are hard to answer, that are slow to be answered, or that seem never to be answered, don't make the mistake in thinking that those questions unmake God. Those questions show our limits, not his"—and Thom absorbed the words, appreciated them even, but his head still itched, and he wanted nothing more than to run his hand through his hair, to put his right index nail on the tingling inch of skin, itch of skin, inch of itch, and scratch, scratch, scratch, but he was bent on his campaign to resist scratching—to embody that Müller resolve—so he narrowed his eyes toward the preacher, toward the far-off microphone, and he saw words as much as he saw anything: black microphone—"I believe in patience!"—red curtain all the way back—"and you need to have drawers of your own, like the questioning young woman, to put those hard questions in"—itch moving from head to a tingling gnaw at his neck—"and you get out your masking tape, and you get out your sharpie"—then the hollow of his ear—"and you write *waiting for new light* on the drawer"—where do we get the word *itch* anyway? verb, noun, probably noun first, skin pricklings more like it, a prickling, pricklings on head, neck, ear hollow, left shin, right side—"and you don't worry about the drawer, and you open it sometimes when some new light has been cast on one of the old tough questions, because truth illuminates. Remember, belovéd, truth illuminates all the questions, but me up here, you down there, we are not the truth. We have truth in us, but we are not the truth, and we can only do so much, but God can illuminate all, and he will use you and me to illuminate some things to some people, but you don't know all of his ways, I don't know all of his ways, but I know that truth shines, illuminates, and I know that if you search after truth, you will get answers, but I don't know when they'll come or how they'll come, but if you stop searching for the truth, then what chance do you have of finding it? You can think of faith as leaping toward God if you like. You can think of faith as a leap. But I like to think of faith as a type of patience too, and you don't always have to leap, belovéd. Sometimes enduring is enough."

For years after his brother's death, Thom had nightmares. Sometimes he was on the bridge trying to talk him down. Sometimes he was standing on the water below waiting to catch him. Always failing. Always failed. Words trying as best they can but the jump always happened. Limbs exerting beyond their bounds but always bringing him a few feet too far this way or not enough that way to receive the tender body, which fell still and silent. But other nightmares placed Thom in his brother's body as he fell, and there was no one beside him at the top of the bridge. No one delivering words that might have been enough. And there was no one at the bottom to run toward him and fix it all. No one there to undo it with some miraculous feat. And as he fell, he was not still or silent. He was screaming. He was flailing. He was thinking as Evan, and he was thinking as Thom. And he was picturing his bedroom, wondering if he should have made his bed and cleaned his room before he drove off. And he was thinking of the unanswered phone calls and the voicemails he left, one to the girl, *This is what I'm doing*, and one to the best friend, *I want you to have my things*, and one to the brother, *This is not your fault*, but the brother was out, always out, and far away, and to him it was always his fault, every time he experienced it again, and he drove the car to the middle of the bridge and left it in traffic, and he didn't leave much time for anyone to do any talking, and he acted quickly, too quickly, he knew, because that was the only way it could happen, and it was a nightmare for each of them every time, and it was such a slow quickness, and there were so many lives unfolding and unfolding and unfolding as he was falling, so many lives that could be so different based on the slightest things, one of the three answering perhaps, or the girl not breaking it off just yet, or the boy realizing that she moved on and will move on even after he did this, and he would have too. He would have moved on too. And Thom as Evan thought that while falling. Every time. And he thought hundreds of other things. *Older brother is favorite brother.* Not true, sweet brother, not true. *She is my soul mate and life is nothing without her.* Not true, sweet brother, not true. *I am strange and awkward and alone and alone and alone, and I don't want to be falling anymore, and please stop this and please save me and please save me, and I'm sorry and Oh God I'm sorry and Oh God I'm sorry*—"Come back," Thom screamed, and he gripped the chair in front of him, and he saw that there was a chair in front of him, and people around him attended to him, the man in front turning around and saying, "It's okay, brother," the man beside him putting a hand on his shoulder and squeezing, saying, "It will pass. It takes time to get it out of your system." And his hand was large and strong and calloused, and Thom felt like a child beside him, and Thom said, "I'm okay. Thank you." And the two men nodded. And others around him smiled, and then they all turned back to look at the preacher way down up front.

"And if you are a sarcastic person," the preacher said, "you might say, so what? What is the point of togetherness in a bad situation, in a situation with a dismal outlook? So the boat has tipped over, and we're in the middle of the ocean, and we are thrashing about, and we are afraid of drowning. There's no land in sight. And you're saying, 'At least we're all in this together out here. That's good? We're drowning out here, but at least we're in it as a team. Is that supposed to comfort me?' And I say, yes, that should provide some comfort, but you know what, that's just a small part of it. Here's the comfort. I've been in that ocean of doubt. And folks out here, seated all around you, they've been in that ocean of doubt. And I didn't drown, and they didn't drown, but you can't experience their rescue exactly as they did. Hey, I'd give you my life preserver if I could. And I'll give you this Bible in my hand, and I'll direct you to passages, and I'll pray with you, but what I'm saying to you is that each of our life preservers is made a bit differently, and I can't save you from an ocean of doubt, but oh I want to help you, and I want to help your unbelief, and I want others all around you to help your unbelief, but we can't do the saving, just the encouraging, just the directing."

The nightmares lessened, but they never went away, and Thom doubted they ever would. Did the girl have nightmares still? he often wondered, or the best friend? With his parents, Thom learned it was better not to bring things up himself. To wait for them. And in the beginning of coming to grips with it all, they cried, and laughed a little, but mostly cried all the time, and Thom managed to finish school but he slipped below *summa*, then *magna*, then *cum laude* all together, flying back and forth during his junior and senior years as often as he could, and he managed to keep things going with his girl, and he managed to get a job, and he managed to smile now and again, and he saw his parents managing, and he managed a marriage, and Julie managed to deal with him through it all, his waking and his screaming and his sweating. And one day during the pregnancy Thom heard Julie say, "Let's name her Ayva," and Thom said, "That's beautiful. Sure." But when he saw his wife spell the name out weeks later, only then did he realize her gesture. *Eva*, she'd spelled it. *Eva*. And then the nightmares started again before they went away for a while, but he told her he liked the name because he did like the sound and he liked her gesture and he was getting used to the spelling all the time while all the time wondering if that was a helpful thing—to have a child named *Eva*.

The preacher paused, and then he walked to one side of the stage, set his Bible down on a little table, and then walked back to the center, gripping the microphone now with two hands. "You know, belovéd," he said. "All this talk of water has put something on my heart. I want to hold a baptism today. I want to hold baptisms today. It's been a while since we've done this. I was going to hold an altar call today. I was going to ask people to come up who wanted to dedicate their lives to Christ. And if that's you, then please see me after the service and we'll say a prayer together. But all this talk about water has me thinking about one of our great symbols of dedication. One of our great symbols of rejuvenation. This is no small commitment. This is not for you strong Christians out there who have done this. In some traditions, baptism is a one-time deal. And I think that's mostly true. Don't come walking up here if I baptized you last year. I want to see those folks who have walked up here for an altar call on a Sunday two weeks ago, two months ago, two years ago. I want to see the new believers who haven't taken the next step. I want you to feel cleansing waters over you. I want you to have this experience, this symbol."

The preacher motioned to a group of people sitting down front and off to the side, and they started walking up and some of them picked up instruments and microphone stands that had been leaning on a wall, and they gathered at the front of the stage around the preacher. "The praise band will play now, and let's all sing loudly together to the glory of God, and let's support the people who decide to get baptized today. Elder Davis and Elder Packs will help me prepare the baptismal, and I invite you all to stand and sing as many songs as we need to. As we get to. We could sing all day, couldn't we?"

And one of the singers on stage said, "Amen!"

And the preacher walked to the back of the stage and drew back the red curtain, and there was a large clear tub sitting on top of the once-hidden part of the stage, and even in the back row Thom could see the tub filling with water, two men—two elders—standing on each side, having turned a knob from somewhere to let the water in. "I'm waiting back here for those who are ready for this commitment. You all sing. Sing to the glory of God, and I will meet the believers ready for the next step back here." The preacher handed his microphone to one of the singers, and he walked to the clear tub behind the musicians, and the praise band struck up, and the singers bellowed, and drums and cymbals tapped from a corner, and guitars blared, and hands clapped and clapped and clapped, and words from a song Thom didn't know rose up and out and in—"If I, *If I*, had ten thousand hands, I'd use them, *use them*, all to lift his name"—and the congregation all seemed to know the words even though there was no program or hymnal or projected text for anyone to see. Unlike tomorrow when he and Julie would attend Monday chapel at the Episcopal high school up in the hills his parents sacrificed so much to send their boys to, where tomorrow Thom and the other reunion visitors would be acknowledged, where tomorrow he and Julie would stand side by side together singing from the same hymnal.

In the course of ten minutes or so, three people walked up to be baptized. And Thom watched them get submerged—a woman, a man, a woman—and with each the preacher was waist deep in the tub, in his suit, probably with his keys and his wallet and all his clothes things in his pockets still. Thom had waited for him to empty his pockets before he climbed in, but he didn't. And he lovingly held each of their heads like an infant's head before he directed them backward into the water. And he embraced each one, and he said words to them before and after, and Thom wanted to know the words, but he did not want to walk up there to find out, and he desired to experience the sensation they had felt. He suspected the water was cool. But how cool? And he knew the feeling of rising out of a pool and having the water spill down the head and race down the back and other skin parts, and he knew the feeling of air meeting skin that just had water on it before falling to the ground, and he knew the feeling of rubbing his eyes after a daily shower and clearing away the drops so he could open his eyes and take in what's there waiting to be seen, and was it all the same up there? And it couldn't be because they each left the tub in their clothes, and they were handed a towel by either Elder Davis or Elder Packs, but their clothes were still soaking, and they each rubbed the towel on their faces first and then attended to their bodies, but their clothes had looked heavy as the first two walked up the aisle to their seats, and the third one had come closest to Thom, sitting three rows in front of him, and when she got back to her row, she stood for a second so that those closest to the aisle could scoot out to let her in, and while she stood a puddle formed at her shoes, water that had saturated her jeans and sweater slowly moving downward in thick togetherness until the weight reached the point that it could fall off the clothing, the bottom rim of the sweater, the cuffs of the jeans, and before she went to her seat, she mopped the puddle, rubbing her towel on the red painted cement floor, and then she slid into the row and put the towel on the floor and stood over it singing and clapping, her clothes sagging all around her.

And then a fourth person began the walk down the aisle from one of the middle rows, and Thom watched as he had watched the others, and Thom wished he could follow behind the person, and Thom had been baptized as a baby, and what did that feel like? and what did his little infant self-do when the minister sprinkled water on his tiny baby head, droplets clinging to his soft hair, pooling together at the roots, probably not running down his head if it was a light sprinkling, and did he feel it? He must have. And did he shiver, did he cry, did he feel different, and did his parents feel different? And he couldn't even remember his brother's baptism, when Thom would have been two or three depending on the month, and did he stand up there beside his brother while the minister baptized Evan with a sprinkling on his tender head, or did his mother or father hold him because he was too shy to stand before the whole congregation, and Thom knew that baptism was a one-time deal for the Methodists, and the Presbyterians, and the Catholics, and probably lots of others, and he hoped it helped Evan, but *hoped* is not the right word there, and *helped* is not the right word there, but when Thom found himself praying for Evan, he sometimes thought that it was a good thing that Evan was baptized before he died, and he thought, *Sweet brother, what were you thinking?* and he thought, *Sweet brother, I will see you again no matter what anyone says,* and he thought, *But what if I don't see him?* and he thought, *Sweet brother, sweet brother, sweet brother, I will see you again no matter what anyone says,* and Thom could not stand his chair any longer, so he stood up, and he had managed to forget about his body for so long, about his skin for so many minutes, but there was the itch on his head, and in the hollow of his ear, and everywhere, everywhere pricklings of skin, skin prickling as an annoyance, as a hindrance, but as something he could tough out, and now that he was standing, the back of his thighs itched and prickled, and he slid himself out of his row, past the legs of people closer to the aisle, and the fourth person was walking toward the tub, nearing the stage, ascending the stage stairs, hugging the preacher, stepping on a stepstool by the tub, one leg in, then the other leg in, and then leaning back, and then the weight of his head given to the strong hand of the preacher, and then submerged backward, and then the clapping from the congregation coming behind Thom as he'd somehow climbed the stage stairs, and then a towel was handed to the person—to the woman—who went fourth, and now Thom was at the tub, and now the preacher's eyes were brown, and his head was not as round as Thom had thought it was from way back there, and he said to Thom, "I'm Pastor Larry," and Thom said, "I want to feel what it's like," and Pastor Larry said, "Do you call yourself a Christian?" and Thom said, "I do," and Pastor Larry said, "Do you call yourself a believer," and Thom said, "I do. But I know I need to set my unbelief aside. I need to do that," and Pastor Larry said, "Belovéd man, will you seek to follow Christ in all that you do?" and Thom said, "I will," and Pastor Larry said, "Have you been baptized before?" and Thom said, "I've not felt the water pour over me, but I want to."

Pastor Larry motioned for Thom to get into the tub, and Thom climbed the step stool and hoisted one leg over the rim and into the water, and then the other leg, and now he stood waist deep in the tub, and the water was lukewarm, not at all cold, and it was pleasant to be in, but Thom thought that it should be crisp and sharp and that he should be made to tough out cold water for some reason. Pastor Larry stood right next to Thom now, and he wrapped a strong arm around his waist and he cupped his other hand at the back of Thom's head, and he whispered, "You'll want to plug your nose on the way back," and Thom brought his right hand up to cup his mouth and pinch his nose, and Pastor Larry looked at him and nodded, and his face was grave—both flat and tense—and Thom felt the strength of his arms and his body pressed beside him, and Thom let himself relax in the warm grip of this man, and Pastor Larry boomed, "I baptize you in the name of the Father and of the Son and of the Holy Spirit," and Thom's skin fluttered as he was plunged backward and back and neck and head and another's hand broke the water, and water licked neck, then ears and cheeks, and nose and lips and his own hand, and water collected in his eyebrows and head hair so that when his direction was reversed and he was shot up out of the collected warmth, the drops that happened to be sliding together around his eyebrows and head hair stayed on him longer than the droplets on his skin that fell back to the mass of warmth in the tub, and then he was standing, and then he saw light as one hand and then the other rubbed his eyes open, and Pastor Larry embraced him and said, "We'll have a certificate for you after the service," and then he turned to another standing outside the tub, and one of the elders grabbed his hand to help him out of the tub, and then one leg went over, and then the other leg went over, and then the other elder handed him a towel—it was purple—and Thom heard the praise band playing and singing, and they were clapping, and one singer said, "All right!" as he walked by her and descended the stage stairs.

He patted his face in the towel as he walked up the aisle toward the back of the sanctuary, and he looked straight ahead only but was aware of smiles and cheers coming at him from the congregation split on either side of him, and some hands patted his back and arms or squeezed his arms, and he smiled but kept walking straight ahead, and kept walking until he pushed the theater doors open and made it into the theater lobby, and it was empty, no greeter this time, and he pushed his way through the glass doors with brass handles, and he met the outside air with the biting sharpness he'd expected to find in the tub's waters, and he felt the keys of his rental car in his heavy pants, and he would sit in the car all wet and think about what he'd just done, and then he would drive back to the airport, where he had landed not long ago, and he would park a few blocks away until ten minutes after Julie's plane was scheduled to land, and then he would circle her terminal until he found her standing outside expecting him, her one carry-on beside her. He would meet her where she was. He would meet her where she had been for a short while, hop out with the car running and trunk popped, and before they embraced their safe arrivals, and before she asked him why he was soaking and shivering, he would grab her bag and throw it beside his, his wetness bleeding into the bag's canvas and whatever else came near him.

the butcher's tale

Here's a story. I heard it from an old timer the other day after we showed up at the bus stop at the same time, with the bus having just pulled out and left us, so we sat on the bench, me in my apron, but I didn't know I had the damned thing on, and him in his itchy looking scarf even though it was warm. And he said to me, "A butcher, eh?"

And I looked down at my stained apron, and I thought about taking it off, but I didn't because I was tired and comfortable off my feet, so I said, "Yeah." I didn't have anything to follow up with, because what could I say— An old man, eh?—and of course I could see he was an old man, and I guess I could have asked about what he used to do, but why bother? I was tired and he was whatever he used to be.

But then he started talking about this or that, and then he said, "Listen." And that got me. He had my attention then. I was listening. So he said, "Listen. I want to tell you a story. A story to pass the time until the next bus gets here."

I said, "Ok."

And he said something like this. I didn't interrupt him. I listened. He said, "There was a guy who was a recluse, an old man, and the townspeople said that he was a wise man, or a holy man, a thinker who chose the solitary life out there in his house, which was on a mild hill surrounded by hedges, plants, and trees that were not quite overgrown but not tidy either, and he would visit the town once a week, sometimes twice a week, to buy the things he needed, like apples and paper, and the townspeople treated him with reverence, nodding to him in the streets, getting him his things in the stores and taking his money, but not pressing him with questions, not trying to extract the wisdom they knew to be in him, strolling through his veins, knocking about his head, but the children didn't buy it, and the children jeered at him as he passed by, flicking pebbles at his brown leather boots, whispering their laughter at the dullness of his brown leather hat and his brown leather satchel, and one day one of the older kids said to the rest of the towns children, 'I'm going to prove that he's a stupid old man,' and he told them his plan, which was to hide a bird behind his back as he knocked on the old man's door and then ask him, once he opened the door, 'What do I have behind my back?' and if somehow the old man guessed it, or sensed it, and he was able to say, 'A bird,' then the boy would ask, 'And is this bird dead or alive?' and if the old man said, 'It's dead,' then the boy would prove him wrong by pulling out the live bird and they would all laugh at him, but if the old man said, 'It's alive,' then the boy would snap the bird's neck behind his back and prove him wrong by pulling out the dead bird and they would all laugh at him."

And the old man on the bench, not the one in the story, the old man on the bus bench paused for a few seconds after talking through most of the story so far. And maybe he was remembering how the next part went, or maybe he just needed to rest his throat. But I didn't say anything because he really had me at this point. I was really wondering how this would all play out.

So the old man on the bus bench, the one next to me, he started up again about the old man in the story, and he said, "So the kids followed the older boy to the old man's house, and the older boy knocked on the door while the rest of the towns children looked on behind him. And the old man opened the door, and he didn't look surprised or concerned at the crowd of gathered children. And behind his back, the boy had the bird cupped in one hand and sealed with the other, and he said his line, 'What do I have behind my back?' And the old man looked straight ahead at the boy's face, which is said to have been flat but with a mischievous lip, and the old man saw in his right peripheral, just through the crowd of children in the background, a white feather near the walkway to his house. So the old man answered, 'You are holding a white bird.' There were gasps behind the boy, but the boy was unfazed, and he delivered his second question, asking, 'Is the bird dead or alive?' And the old man looked at him for a long heartbeat, and he said to him slowly, heavily, 'The answer to that question is in your hands.'"

Now I'd been looking straight ahead as he was telling it. I was absorbing it, seeing everything he was saying, but when the old man on the bench finished, when he said, "The answer to that question is in your hands," which is what the wise old man in his story ended with, when all that was done and there was a pause, I looked towards the old man on the bench, having been pulled out of all I was seeing, being pulled back into this world, and the old man was serious looking, real serious, and he even grabbed my arm for emphasis, the way old people do sometimes, the way they want to touch you, cling to you, while they're talking.

And I said, "That's a good story," and he smiled kind of proudly, and we were quiet until another bus came and we boarded and left each other's company inside. He got that story from somewhere. It's written somewhere, but I don't know where, but it's circulating, like this, making its rounds, though always a bit different in its details I'm sure, but the story is the same story in its essence, and I suppose it's a moral. I suppose we listeners walk away and think about our choices and our power, maybe our intentions. I don't know. Something like that. We are supposed to think, to consider the lesson, which is a deep one, to be sure, but this a partial story, a beginning really, and the ending is always better than the beginning in a story with any weight to it. I know that much. And I know this thing's not done. When he had told this story to others, however, many times over however many years, did the listeners wonder what happened next? Most didn't, I bet, but they should. Did they wonder if the boy relented? Did they imagine him growing frustrated, revealing the bird only to snap its neck after all and storm off as some young boys do when they've been bested, or did they imagine him releasing the bird, laughing at his own ignorance, his own blindness or misguided intention, laughing at himself, who was then a better and improved self, laughing in relief as he released the bird and felt the wind from its first flaps flitter his cheek skin while the symbol of power, of delicacy, of pride, love and hate, acceptance, and so much else, took off in majesty?

But I know better because I'm a butcher. I'm a reader—I read too— and I watch the good movies, the films that press us a bit more—I like to watch those ones at home as well as the more popular ones in the theaters sometimes—but really I know that's not the ending because I'm a butcher, because the day after I heard that story, when there was new light again and I was up again early and I was in the shop early, I had in front of me a duck—a lot of ducks stacked to the side—but there was the duck in front of me, the one I was holding. And I'm holding it, and I've got my big hand around its narrow neck. It's so narrow when it's just skin when all the feathers are gone, and it's so delicate, and this is a duck, much bigger than whatever the boy in the story was holding behind his back. I'm guessing it was a white dove. That seems like the kind of bird for that story. But I'm holding this duck's neck, my right hand encircling its delicate skin. And the duck was already dead when it came to me, but I'm pretending it's alive. I'm pretending I'm the boy in the story, and I put the duck behind my back. The bulk of its rubbery skin, the main weight of it, its roundness, is nestled into the open palm of my left hand behind me, and its legs dangle over my fingers, its little flipper feet dangling off those skinny legs, and my right hand is still around its neck, and I'm alone in the back room. I'm next to the bigger chopping table, and I don't even have the knives out yet for the day, just the ducks, and I close my eyes, and I walk through the story, and I pretend I'm the boy, and I see myself standing in front of the closed door of the old man's house. And I need to knock, but I'm holding this duck behind me, and I'm pretending it's alive and I'm pretending the skin feels like feathers, and I'm pretending that the coolness is a warmth and that my heartbeat is matching that of the delicate bird's behind me. But I need to knock, but my hands are full, so how did the boy knock? He must have used his foot. So I use my foot to kick the door in front of me. And my foot finds a leg of the chopping table, and it's a sturdy leg, so I kick it, but now it's a front door because I'm still closing my eyes and imagining. And I kick the door two more times, and it opens and there's the old man in the story, who looks a lot like the real old man from the bus bench except he's all in brown and grey and he's scarfless. I say my first line and the old man says, "A white bird," and I know he must be cheating because how can he see. This bird is behind my back, after all. So I say my second line, and I am so determined to make him slip up for some reason. For some reason, I am really wanting to show him to be a fool, and I am waiting for him to say one of two things. I am waiting for him to say, "It's dead" or "It's alive." I can't think beyond those two phrases. Those are the only fair answers. One or the other. Choose. And he is taking forever. And my heart is pounding, so the bird's heart must be pounding, and all of a sudden I want him to say, "It's dead." I want him to say it so badly because

I want this bird to live all of a sudden. All of a sudden, that's what I want, for this bird to live. And if he says, "It's dead," I can let the thing loose. We can all watch it flit away with its hollow warmness. And my muscles are tense. And I'm waiting, and I'm waiting, and out of nowhere he says, "The answer to that question is in your hands," and I'm thinking, not fair but whatever. At least I can let this wonderful stupid thing go, I guess, and I'm about to bring the bird out just to be done with it all. I'm about to whip the bird around with my hand cupping its mass, but I feel then that my hand encircling its neck is too tight. There's practically no space in there, in the grip of my right hand, just enough space for the thinnest of skin, a tube of flesh wrangled while I was nervous. Wrangled while I was waiting. The boy squeezed. I tried not to have the boy squeeze. But he did. And it doesn't matter what the boy thinks of the clever man's response. It doesn't matter if the clever man wants to teach him something. Because our poor boy will kill the bird every time before the answer is given. Because the answer is always too late. At least for this bird. At least for this choice. And that's the way it is. And that's the way that things like that end.

chrysalis

When you eat the caterpillar, be careful not to crush it with your teeth. You must be delicate. You must allow the little thing to settle into your warm, open mouth before you close it. You must cage it behind your teeth so that it thinks inching its way down your throat and nestling itself in your stomach was its own idea.

Begin by placing the caterpillar on your palm. Do not shrink if it tickles. Do not cup your hand. Your palm is now its platform. Keep it straight, and bring the caterpillar and its platform to the space between your chin and lower lip. Then open your mouth as wide as you can. And make sure your tongue is flattened on your mouth's floor. Your mouth has a roof and a floor, of course, but it also has a rug, delicate and textured, enticing for its subtle pattern of soft pinks, an area rug perfectly measured. Unroll your gentle rug for your caterpillar. Hide your lower teeth behind your lower lip. This will be tricky with your mouth stretching upward. Press the tip of your tongue to the back of your lower teeth. Now your lip is a step leading to the home of your mouth. And after that step is your rug. Keep it flat and enticing. It might take a little while for the caterpillar to come inside. You must be patient. The caterpillar will see that the platform it's on is flat and hopeless. The caterpillar will want to climb the step of your lip, to find such soft habitation.

It's important to select a caterpillar nearing the pupal stage. A young caterpillar is a ravenous thing. It will tear at your soft pink rug, and as it inches down your throat it will snack on your esophagus the whole way, inch by inch, bite by bite, until it discovers the feast of your stomach lining, devouring and devouring until it is gorged and ready to rest, blanketing itself as a little doll. So choose a hoary caterpillar, plump from leaves and other stuff, plump and ready for its nap. There are many to choose from, and you will learn which ones you like. You'll need to grow a tolerance for it charging all sides of your esophagus as it inches down, its curiosity directing it to the abbey below, where it finds its brethren living peaceful and productive days, some wrapped up in sleep, some flittering, their thin wings hammering the walls so that every moment is like the moment you first saw her.

thursday morning at a. r. valentien

Greg began scooping out the butter with the melon baller. He placed each little yellow globe in the center of one of the butter dishes, which were bright blue and square in shape. After thirty minutes of this, he had filled up five trays with a couple dozen dishes on each. He was grateful that the night crew had remembered to fill the trays with the clean empty dishes and roll the tray dock over to the butter fridge. He was the first busboy on that day, and someone else would be showing up soon. "Busboy," he said. The kitchen was large and quiet. And clean. It was always clean in the morning. "Middle-aged busboy. Forty-two-year-old busboy." He walked over to the coffee brewers and poured himself another cup. This summer job would be over in a few weeks. Just when he had started getting efficient, he thought. He took his coffee through the kitchen doors and into the restaurant's main dining area. He stood in the center, sipping from the cup amid unset tables. Through the windows, the morning sky was still dark.

Back in the kitchen, there was a rustling of someone else pouring coffee. The other busboy had arrived. Greg turned to see Trevor enter the dining area, a styrofoam cup between his palms.

"You're not supposed to use those cups," joked Trevor.

Greg smiled. He liked working with Trevor. "When you're an old man like me," said Greg, "you'll appreciate the porcelain."

"All right, professor," Trevor said. "You're not so old yet."

"Why do you guys say that? Professor. It's getting old now."

"But it's true, right? Classes start up soon. And then you'll be gone, right? Back to bigger and better things."

"It's not really true. Well. No, no, it's not really true." Greg took a sip and set the cup back on the saucer cupped in his left palm. "Instructor. Technically."

Trevor had begun straightening some of the chairs. "Let's go get the tablecloths," he said. "Is the butter done?"

The pair walked out of the dining room together and into an employees-only hallway that connected to the lodge. A. R. Valentien was the costly restaurant inside The Lodge at Torrey Pines, but it had its own outside entrance so that the La Jolla and San Diego locals could patronize it as well. Greg and Trevor carried stacks of pressed tablecloths from the hotel's laundry room back to the restaurant—the same laundry room where they dropped off and picked up their uniforms at least twice a week. They put the tablecloths on all the inside tables, using squirt bottles with warm water to flatten out the creases, and then they set out the napkins, silverware, saucers, coffee cups, bread plates, and stemmed water glasses. When they finished the inside, the two opened up a pair of French doors to the patio overlooking the pool and then began to set the outside tables. The early light shone now, and below the patio other employees were pulling out the poolside furniture and drawing back the canvas openings of the poolside tents.

"So what did she say?" Greg asked. "Your girlfriend. What did she say this time?"

"She still thinks you're wrong. She says she can't explain it yet, but she's researching it. She says she knows it's wrong. It feels wrong to her."

A few days back Trevor had pulled out a picture of himself with his girlfriend to show Greg. They were on the beach in front of Scripps Pier. She was going to be a freshman at UCSD, Trevor explained, where he had hoped to transfer after another year at City. Greg had turned the photograph over, and where Trevor had written "Sheila and me" in pencil she had used a pen to strike through the "me" and write in an "I" beside it.

"Did you explain what I said about cases?" Greg now asked. "Did you tell her what I said about constituents in and out of context?"

"I did," said Trevor. "I mean I tried to. I think I said it right. I don't really care anymore." He swiveled around a coffee cup so that the handle angled correctly. "It doesn't matter."

"It matters. Sheila and me is fine. Words on the back of a photograph."

Greg set down another water glass. "There's no grammatical context. Sheila and me. Why not? Why not write down Sheila and me? Is there confusion? I don't think so. Is the meaning clear? Of course, it is." Greg grabbed more glasses off a cart they had rolled out. With his palm up he spread his fingers out and one by one slipped ten glass stems between his fingers, sliding each new glass base beneath two others. With the ten glasses dangling from his hand he walked over to another table. "You should care. You're dating a hyper-corrector. One who doesn't understand how language works. One who loves rules. Even if she doesn't get why they are so. That's the problem there, I think. She sees things as right and wrong. There's no fluidity there. Tell her that language is fluid. You tell her that. Tell her that language isn't stagnant."

"Sure," Trevor said.

"It's called prescriptivism," said Greg. "You're a smart kid. Too smart to be like that."

As Greg and Trevor were finishing up outside, a few of the cooks had already arrived in the kitchen, chopping vegetables and doing other prep work. And then the waiters and food runners arrived too. Once the busboys finished their prep work, their job was mostly to stay out of the way until diners began showing up. Greg and Trevor went into the small private dining room and began folding napkins. The large table was set, but when the room was not in use the busboys often gathered there to get work done while staying out of the kitchen. Greg could tell that Trevor was over the me-versus-I conversation, so after suggesting he write in "This is a picture of" directly above the "Sheila and me" now changed to "Sheila and I," he decided to let it go until another shift, adding a final "Let me know what she says then. Be sure to tell me what she thinks of that."

Diners began arriving, and Greg and Trevor greeted them first, venturing out to different tables, setting down a blue butter dish near the centerpiece, picking up each water glass and filling it up with the pitcher kept at an appropriate distance from the diner, and then offering choices of finely sliced breads, using the tongs to drop down the appropriate type and number from the platter onto each bread plate. Then they'd be gone, letting the waiters step in but still eyeing the water glasses and bread plates for potential refills, and eyeing the plates of the main dishes after the food runners would drop them off, wanting to clear them away as soon as each diner was finished. After they'd provided the water and bread for a few tables each, the manager approached them as they stood along a back wall and told them to prepare the small dining room. Greg and Trevor went to the room and began removing stacks of folded napkins, placing them into various built-in cupboards here and there throughout the main dining area. The pair met back in the private dining room and tinkered with the settings, sliding a glass this way, straightening out a knife just so. The table was rectangular and sat twelve.

"Who do you think it is?" said Greg.

"I've no idea," Trevor said. "I haven't heard about anyone checking in. Nick Cage was here last week, but he checked out already."

"I heard about that. Never saw him, though."

"Me neither."

"I guess he gave Davis a hundred dollar tip. For juice and eggs." Trevor pulled down on his vest. "You know, you'd probably be a waiter in a few months if you stayed on. You know, kept working while you still taught. Rich says I can start running food at the end of the summer. Maybe get some night shifts added to my schedule."

"I can't work nights," Greg said. "The kids."

"Oh yeah. Well, maybe a day shift or two. The tips would help."

"Rich already asked if I'd stay on. He knows I'm gone in three weeks. I've got a five-five on three campuses lined up for the year. Two at City, you know. This fall. Two at City. I'll have some office hours there. I'll tell you when. You can pop in and say hi now and then."

The manager walked into the small dining room and told them to set up an outside table instead, to push a six-top around the side of the patio. Greg and Trevor went outside and removed all the settings from one of the large circular tables. Then they lifted it off the floor a bit and shuffled around a bend of the patio to a secluded spot where they sometimes set up an outside table or two. They walked back to retrieve the settings, and then they reset the table and brought over the six chairs. They went inside, and the manager met them there, and he told Greg to take the private table and Trevor to keep an eye on the rest. And then he left, and Greg and Trevor remained along the back wall, standing silently and taking note of water lines, and the manager returned again into the main room, leading a family behind him, guiding them slowly toward the French doors and around the side of the patio to where their table had been set up.

"It's Reba McEntire," Greg whispered to Trevor. "It's Reba."

"The TV star."

"No, no," Greg hushed. "The country singer."

Reba and her troop sat down at the private table, and then Greg grabbed a pitcher of ice water and walked over to them and filled their glasses.

For the first time in his eleven-week stint at A. R. Valentien, Greg envied the servers. No, not the servers, just Jimmy. Economics major, fifth or sixth year senior, and now the server chosen by head manager Richard Crimsly to wait on the McEntire-Blackstock table. Greg stood in the backdrop while Jimmy was saying something to them. Perhaps the juices, Greg thought. So many juices to choose from.

When Greg had filled her water glass earlier, Reba said a faint "Thank you," and Greg had lingered for a small moment, catching a glimpse of her pale thighs beneath her tan shorts. So ordinary, those shorts. And the white of her skin should not have surprised him, but it did, and before he had stayed at her thighs for that long second, he had dared to take in her face while in the slow process of setting down her newly-filled water glass before she said that "Thank you." And her eyes had not been looking at him while he considered the brownness of her red hair and her husband Narvel had not been looking at him while he set down his glass and determined that he was not disappointed by that brownness. Nor had their children seemed to notice him as he filled up and set down their glasses while contemplating their stepmother-mother's un-made-up skin around her eyes and contrasting everything to the poster in his bedroom twenty-five years ago in 1980 when she was married to the great steer wrestler Charlie Battles and he, soon to graduate from high school and younger than all but one of these children now appeared to be, would have attended college in Oklahoma if his parents had been willing to pay for out-of-state tuition. But now Jimmy was through talking to them for the moment, and he approached Greg and told him that he had forgotten to offer them bread while pouring the water.

"I'm sorry, Jimmy. I'll do it now," said Greg. "I'll tell them about the breads." And he grabbed the platter off the nearby station, but Jimmy had told him not to bother—that he had told them about the breads but they were just going to wait for their breakfasts. So Greg stood alone while Jimmy went back to the kitchen, and he could see Trevor meandering through the main patio area, first with his pitcher and then with his tray of sliced bread.

But Greg remained where he could see Reba's table, watching the figures at a side-glance while his head faced the golf course in the distance.

The food runners brought out the Blackstocks' food quickly. Greg watched Reba's water line but it never got low enough to warrant a visit. They ate and spoke about things while Greg maintained his side-glance. He imagined they would visit the beach today, Del Mar or La Jolla Shores. Perhaps later Reba would get some shopping in while Narvel played a round of golf. And she would be put together then, rouged lips and cheeks and darkened eyes. Striking, for sure, Greg thought, but not as satisfying as this private glimmering, the rare glimpse of Reba in the morning, Reba waiting for breakfast, Reba eating breakfast, Reba unguarded while the day progresses yet seems not to have begun at all. Then came the point in the meal Greg disliked the most, the point when eating slowed but plates remained somewhat full. When people finished their food completely, Greg would swoop in and stack plates in the crook of his arm as well as any of the other bussers now. Or when their plates still had food but were pushed to the side. That, too, was a good scenario. But Reba's plate and two of her kids' plates sat partially eaten and in the same spot where the runners had left them. He watched straight on now. He had to stare now to do his job. Were they picking, he thought. No. No, they must be done. So he began to walk toward their table, and he tried to push out of his mind the rude women from three days ago and from four weeks ago who each snapped at him when he attempted to remove a plate with some morsel or other still on it without asking first since he was not supposed to if he could help it.

He picked up the three empty plates, and Narvel gave him a nod, and then he grabbed the other two children's mostly-finished plates, and no one griped about not being finished, and then he approached Reba and realized that he should have come to her first, and he worried she would think him rude, but she smiled as he reached in cautiously for her plate while balancing the five others, and when the plates were ready to be taken back to the kitchen and when his time with her would have to be over, he stayed beside her—a woman who marries bearded men named Charlie Battles and Narvel Blackstock but not the honey-cheeked and slightly younger Greg Finney—and he began to say something, but his throat bleated, and then Narvel said, "We're all set, friend," but Greg kept looking at Reba, and he had to speak and so he said, "*Feel the Fire* and *Heart to Heart* are still my favorites," and Reba said, "Thanks, dear. That's been a while," and Narvel stood up, and the oldest son stood up, and Greg stood beside the sitting Reba as he balanced their plates in his left arm while his right hand sat on the top plate where the yolk from her half-eaten egg was saturating his uniform's white cuff. And the husband and son wore protective looks, their lip lines straight, their eyes squinting slightly, and they remained stationary, seeming to wait for Greg to walk away from Reba, and while Greg admired their protective display and while he did not want them to misunderstand his intentions, he could not walk away from Reba, and he was staring at Reba, and this Reba, the real Reba, was so much more beautiful than the Reba of his youth, the stellar composite of images from the poster in his room and from her album covers, because this was real Reba, and Greg wanted to sit down for coffee with real Reba and explain to her how his marriage had failed, and she could comfort him, and she could reassure him, and while he was staring at Reba, and while Reba was staring at him, and while her husband and oldest son were standing still, waiting for Greg to leave with the dishes piled in his arms and leaning against his chest, while they were there in a quiet moment, Greg said to Reba, "I miss my wife," and after a small second Reba said, "I'm sorry, dear," and Greg waited for more but no one else said anything, and Greg looked at Reba's husband Narvel, and Narvel's protective glare turned sympathetic, his eyes fuller, his lips separating, and he said to Greg, "You'll be okay, friend. Buck up. You'll be okay," and Greg smiled, and he pressed down on the top of the plates with his right hand, bracing the stack as he prepared to walk back to the kitchen, and he said, "Thanks, guys. Thanks, Narvel. Thanks, Reba. You enjoy your stay. Thanks for everything you guys have done," and they both smiled, and their children half-smiled, and Greg walked away, plates and silverware clinking, his right hand smeared in the yolk of Reba's egg, his white cuff yellowed as much as it would yellow, having absorbed everything it could.

Before he clocked out for the day, Greg dropped off his stained uniform at the hotel's laundry room. It would be ready in time for tomorrow's morning shift. He checked in his clean uniform for washing as well in case he decided that he had been subjected to enough embarrassment there. That way, if he had the courage to quit early, he would not have to make an extra trip north and west to return the second uniform. He did that once before, in June when a freshman who had earned a C in his class just weeks earlier had come in with his dad to eat before their tee time. The dad was cordial and oblivious, and the former student was kind enough not to bask in the relishing Greg was sure he felt.

In his car, Greg was not sure where to go. It was not yet one o'clock, but he was tired and defeated and did not want to be home alone before his kids showed up for Thursday dinner. He got them for three-weekday dinners now. And every other Saturday he would take them somewhere. They would be coming at six, brother and sister driving together. Greg would need to put the lasagna in at five. He imagined that he should drive down to one of the beaches and walk solemnly until then. He cringed at the tired image. He hated sand. But gas was expensive. Driving would not do either. He would go somewhere and sit. He would sit, and he would decide not to go back to work tomorrow. He would decide never to go to A. R. Valentien again, and he would be able to manage on little until he started teaching again in the fall. He would go somewhere and sit. He would not go home until five, and he would be happy when his children visited. And he would laugh with them. And maybe he would ask about their mother, and maybe he would call their mother soon. Either way, he would be happy when his children visited, and he would be happy in the morning again, when he would wake in the dark out of habit, forgetting that his uniforms were turned in and that he had decided to be done there, and he would be happy in the crisp morning, and he would not feel young, but he would not feel old either.

his early paintings looked like things

She drove to the gallery early so she could see her son's paintings before the crowds arrived on opening night. She knew he wouldn't be there yet, that he would wait until later in the night to pop out and mingle, that he would get there an hour or two after the doors were opened and then watch from upstairs, take in the reactions before he came down, separating out those who showed up for free wine and something cultural in a city they're not from but claim as their own, separating those out from the people who might be his payers of rent, his payers of groceries, the easers of a mother's mind, this mother, his mother, who is now standing before the first painting in this row, the first mass she'll try to absorb, studying its shapes, its strokes, its colors and its lack of colors. "Look for absence," he once told her. But he was always changing his mind about things. And maybe now he'd tell her something else to look for. She moves toward the placard. No title. She steps back to the center, pulls out a notecard, cupping it in her hand. She reads other sentences, phrases, words he has told her in quick conversations during their Sunday afternoon phone calls, and none of them help her understand him or his painting. Look for this. Consider that. She looks. She considers. She mouths his advice. Her eyes strain. And other people are arriving to look and to consider, and she shoves the notecard back into her purse and engages with the canvas on her own, side-seeing the faces engaged with the same material but armed differently than she is.

His early paintings looked like things: still lifes with fruit and bowls, pitchers and cups. Oh! and the portraits. Such precision. "A God-given talent," she'd tell her son. Oh, how she longs to see those gifts being used. Even to see what he had called his Lucian-Freud phase, the portraits that showed too many brush strokes for her taste, the portraits that seemed to be too aware of their paint, too aware of being collections of strokes, of movements, and not the things themselves. But she'd gladly take those portraits now, the figures that seemed abstractions to her then. She'd hang more of those in her home, gladly, gladly taking down each early canvas if he asked her to, each painting of a thing as a thing, the likenesses of things hung on her living room walls, covering peels in floral paper. She'd take down her dearest paintings in the kitchen even, the ones going back to when he was in grade school if it would mean appendages today, all things at least discernible if not familiar.

Some viewers around her shuffle toward his next one. And she will too in a moment, making the rounds to each canvas, making her way eventually to the gallery owner so that she can write him a check for this first one, and he can place a little round sticker on the placard, indicating its sale, indicating its worth, spurring on the late comers, she hopes, to assist with the needs a mother cannot carry on her own. But for now, she stands a moment longer. Then she inches toward the placard again. A price but still no title. "Titles help," she whispers. She slips a hand into her purse, pincering her card of phrases jotted from his phone calls, from his excited voice explaining what he's creating, but she doesn't pull the card out again, not till later down the line, just runs her fingers over the pen's indentations. She'll let this one hang above her couch, pick it up once his one-month-long show is over, get coached on what to say before her friends sip tea in Christmas mugs, get armed with explanations gifted to her, his payment for her patronage, his easing the mind of one who hates not knowing, of one now readying herself to view the next in line, the next of what is there and what is not there and known not to be there intentionally for one reason or another. But for now she's standing still, this sweet mother, and then her lips move again with his words, his breath, which was once from her but now is his own, which was once from her but now is straining to sustain her poised and viewing self.

williams' letter to the dean

Williams was twenty-four when he started his doctoral program in English. He might be depressed now. He's not sure. His brother struggled with depression throughout high school, but this is new terrain for him. He's recently turned twenty-nine, and as he is walking to his car on the roof of one of the university's many parking structures, he decides that this sadness is temporary and therefore is not technically depression. He's in Ann Arbor, Michigan. But he could be in College Park, Maryland, or Missoula, Montana. He could be in Columbia, Missouri, or Oxford, Mississippi. At any rate, he is at a *University of M*. The town is emblazoned with *M*s. Large block *M*s everywhere. He imagines that College Park, Columbia, and Oxford also think that the letter *M* belongs to them. From his handful of experiences seeing sporting events on TV, he thinks Ann Arbor is the greatest offender. Probably people in Michigan think the *M* belongs to them more than people in Montana think so. And then there's Maine, but he doesn't know what city the University of Maine is in. They probably don't care about *M*s in Maine. Amherst, Massachusetts, probably doesn't care much either, but who knows? And would the Twin Cities care? Are Minnesotans in St. Paul and Minneapolis living in too big of a city to have *M* pride? Williams thinks so. Williams decides that people in small college towns are more likely to love their *M*s. These are some of the thoughts he has. That there are more *University of M*s than any other letter. He doesn't think about the *University of M* cities much—like Memphis—or about the University of Minnesota/Missouri/Michigan/Massachusetts—et cetera, et cetera, and the rest, and the rest—satellite campuses. Just the big *M*s. Just the larger universities. Most states do letter sharing, but the *M* states share the most. Williams is thinking these things because on his way to his parking garage he passed a lot of *M*s—*M*s on signs, *M*s on hats. Even he has been caught in a moment of *M* weakness, purchasing, years ago upon his arrival, a cap with a big *M* on it, though he has yet to wear it out. Let's say that *M* is for Midwest. Let's say that we are in Ann Arbor, Columbia, and the Twin Cities. Let's say that Williams is in Michigan, Missouri, and Minnesota. Not *or*, but *and*. And he is now at once on those three campuses, simultaneously walking, three *Universities of M* among the many *Universities of M*, and here is Williams nearing his car, here in the Midwest, here at a Research 1 institution called *M*, on the roof of a parking garage, and it's a muggy day in late June in the Midwest, and he gets to his car and sees a cluster of bees hovering over the trunk.

Seeing the bees, Williams now knows that the gooey substance someone had squirted on his trunk last night is, in fact, honey. There are dozens of bees floating in a rectangular block built of moving bee bodies. It's not unlike the mayflies rising and falling like pistons in that one Richard Wilbur poem, but these bees are less graceful, less patterned. But at least they are real. Williams drives an 89 Lincoln Town Car, so the honey-plastered trunk provides a wide base for the congregating bees. He is glad to know that the substance is honey, not because honey is better or worse than other things the substance could have been, but because it's always nice to have a question answered. Williams navigates around the wide trunk-turned-bee-paradise over to the driver's side door. The goo that had been smeared on the driver's side window had not attracted any bees. But it looks to be honey also. There was an infant-size diaper stuck to that window this morning. With his shoe, and with his leg balancing awkwardly in front of him, and while thinking, too, that his wife would be surprised by his poise, Williams managed to slide the stubborn diaper down the window, down the door, and onto the street. This was after he rushed out of the house to get to his class on time, the Intro to Fiction Writing class he had reluctantly agreed to teach on a prorated basis.

Williams tosses his bag and phonebook onto the passenger's seat and then shuts his door. He drives out of the parking structure, passing the other roof cars with non-*M* license plates, his fellow graduate teachers and researchers from Florida, California, and just about everywhere between.

The honey on the Lincoln's wide trunk is sun warmed. The honey is so soft and so warm, and the poor bees cannot keep up with it as the car takes it away. They followed buzzingly for a few feet, but now as Williams directs the car down and around the middle levels of the parking structure, the bees are dispersing, flying away to wherever it was they came from.

Williams drives on university streets that turn into city streets. His mind is a wandering mind, and he's aware that people sometimes interpret his vacancy as unintelligence, but he doesn't care about that, and he's a small, quiet person, and he even likes that he's so often misidentified as a good listener—Oh that Williams, such a caring person with his big listening ears, he thinks they think when he's listening before he's not listening—but his mind is not wandering now, and he is alone and he is actively listening as he talks aloud to himself, composing and recomposing the same intangible letter, the same plastic sentences and phrases, this oral artwork whose only fixed unit is its three opening words, Dear Dean Thurman, and he says the opening again, having just taught, now driving home, saying again on this humid day with his windows rolled down and left arm on the door sill, "Dear Dean Thurman," and he waits a moment, pausing for emphasis, sighing for emphasis, thinking then how many of his students' characters sigh before, during, and after dialogue—always sighing so much, their characters, my students' characters, he's thinking—I don't know why they insist on so much sighing, and I almost told Kimberly (or was it Sarah, he's thinking as he's thinking this) that her excessive use of sighs is one of the things that signals to sharp readers that she is a hack—and he would have been reprimanded if he'd said that, but perhaps that would have been good because he could then voice his letter to the dean, and he starts again, saying aloud in the car guiding him home, "Dear Dean Thurman," and he clears his throat, and then he says, "I thought it important for you to know," and his chin rises for this part, "that I did an excellent job. No," and here Williams goes with his pausing again, "a standup job. Teaching the summer section of English 163 despite the fact that I was paid $8.72 an hour for my efforts." Williams would not know the final hourly rate until he finished grading his students' portfolios due the last Friday in July, when the eight-week summer session would come to a close, but ever since he'd agreed to teach the class on a reduced salary because of low enrollment, he kept a little pocket notebook with him and recorded the exact minutes he spent planning each class, grading assignments, answering e-mails, et cetera, and the rest, et cetera. After tallying the minutes for his first three weeks of teaching, he discovered that he had earned $8.72 an hour teaching for the university, teaching as an almost doctor, but not the real kind, mind you. He plans on placing the final hourly rate toward the beginning of the letter when he types it up in a few weeks, right at the beginning for maximum impact. "I am not a person who cares much about money," he goes on, adjusting old lines that had been floating around in his head and composing new ones too, shaping the letter he would mail off in early August, "but I have a wife and child who rely on my salary. Our bills are piling. We rent a nice little red brick house in the northwest part of town." He makes sure he is on the correct road to get to that nice little red brick house. He is. And that's fortunate because he often ends up miles off course when he's thinking while in his car, and now he thinks of Beckett's Lucky thinking, but then he gets himself back to where he was, saying, "We graduate students work hard for very little pay, and I, personally, have never felt underappreciated for my efforts." When he types it up, he will have to think of a stronger phrase than *for my efforts*. "I have never felt underappreciated or taken advantage of," and he wants to be sure this next part is powerful business, and so he says slowly, "until now, that is," and he nods approvingly, "until your office presented me with its absurd ultimatum three days before my class was scheduled to begin." And that will do for now, he's thinking. But he doesn't like thinking things without saying them aloud whenever he's by himself, so he says, "That will do," and saying the thought makes it complete to him in a way that thinking alone doesn't do.

Williams gets to his house, and he's parking the Lincoln along the curb, leaving the narrow driveway open for his wife. He grabs his bag and hurls the phonebook into the backseat. He opens the door, and then he steps on the diaper he'd scraped off the window a few hours earlier, his shoe squishing into the pocket part filled with honey. He kicks the diaper off and walks up to the house, dragging his honey-smeared shoe across his front lawn, his Midwest green lawn. Then he's in the house. Then he's out of the house, his teacher's bag replaced by a bucket of soapy water. And then he sets the bucket and scrub brush down beside the car, and he walks out to the middle of the street where the diaper had landed, and he pulls a plastic grocery bag out of his back pocket, slips it over his hand like a glove, and picks up the diaper. He has seen people do this in the parks while picking up after their dogs. The diaper is a size 1, eight to fourteen pounds. He would not have known that sixteen months ago. He sniffs the puffed-up part that had absorbed the honey, the part that had been stuck to his window last night and then his shoe minutes ago. A diaper filled with honey can mean so many things, Williams is thinking while standing there in the middle of the street. When his wife was pregnant, some of her friends threw her a baby shower, and they all played this tasting game, she and her mom and her sisters, and her friends and their moms, and Williams' mom and other family friends, all these ladies sitting around, using little spoons to sample and then guess the flavors of baby foods poured into clean diapers—This soupy green one tastes like peas, one would say—The mushy brown one like turkey, or, perhaps beef?—and what a riot it was, she said, seeing sweet Aunt Ida, the oldest one there, eating up all the smashed sweet potatoes with her little spoon, imagining, it seemed, that the soft white bowl placed on her lap held the lunch they'd prepared for her. Now Williams' wife and son are driving toward him, and Williams moves out of the street and onto the lawn, wrapping the excess of the plastic bag around the diaper and tying the handles in a knot.

Adria, his wife, steps out of the car, and she surprises Williams by coming to him first, by giving him a tight embrace, and he knows he is foolish, and he knows he is really happy, and her soft body against his is familiar and strange in this quick moment, smelling of lilac or chrysanthemum or something or other, and then she pulls back, squeezes his left arm, and holds his fingertips as she walks back toward the car and then drops them as they separate, him standing on their green lawn, her gliding to the car to unbuckle their sixteen-month-old son from the car seat. And she has the look of an unapproachable woman, pausing there by the car, glancing over at Williams before opening the backseat. Unapproachable because her hair is short and oak-colored, because she is tall in those flats, because she is fit yet shapely, because she smiles only when she means to, and she is not smiling now, and when she is not smiling, the roundness of her cheeks are especially striking, and she was teased as a child because of her prominent cheekbones, the kids telling her she looks like a chipmunk, and when they were dating years ago and she told him that her chipmunk cheeks were one of her insecurities, he said that that was nonsense, that her round cheeks and the way her eyes were set back like that, that that was real beauty, and he told her she looked unapproachable, that she looked too good for him, and besides, he'd said, being short like me is a real insecurity, and he'd said that she belongs in Morrow's for saying that she didn't like her cheeks, and they laughed because that was one of their jokes ever since their date in San Francisco when they walked by Morrow's Nut House and got a kick out of the name. I'm going to drop you off at Morrow's, they say to each other when the days are good and light. And in moments like these when some gesture or comment of hers wipes away familiarity, he is more himself, kinder, more appreciative not just of her but of himself too, as when their relationship was new and delicate, or at least delicate in a different way, when her presence arrested him each time, and when, somehow, he could disable her as well.

Now Adria holds their son, Thomas, and they walk toward Williams on the grass, and Thomas waves to him as sixteen-month olds do, keeping his arm still while bringing his fingertips to the base of his palm. Williams waves back the same way. He and Adria often catch themselves inadvertently waving like that to each other, waving with a slow deliberation that is itself an accomplishment, waving like little children with so many skills still to get a handle on.

They reach Williams, and Williams kisses Thomas and says, "Hey, bud."

Adria stands with her heels close together and her legs perfectly straight, gripping Thomas in the manner he supposes all former ballerinas hold their children. "What's the bucket for?" she asks.

"Need to clean the trunk," says Williams. "Did you see my car this morning?"

"No. Why? What happened?"

"Someone filled up a diaper with honey and stuck it to my window. And then squirted honey all over the trunk. Or I guess it could have happened in the other order."

"You need to report this," Adria says.

"No. It's just some kid," says Williams. "This car can take it. As long as no one messes with your car or the house, I'm not worried."

The car can take it. The paint on the hood, roof, and trunk are sun-faded, each surface with an amoeba-like discoloration, a lighter shade of beige in the center creeping out toward the sides, overtaking its tan original. Williams cares only about the integrity of its body. Not one dent in the old car, his grandfather's old car, and he likes it that way, likes the pristine frame against the seasoned paint job. Back in San José he would get offers for the car. People had wads of cash in their pockets, and they wanted to be seen driving a long rectangular Lincoln without any dents. They probably would have painted it; it probably would have ended up a shiny purple or blue—something flashy, Williams thinks.

"Come in when you're done," says Adria. "Come in and hang out with us."

"I will," says Williams. "I will." And Adria and Thomas head for the house and Williams reaches for the scrub brush by the bucket, soaping the bristles to work on the honey in the same way he worked on the egg stains last week.

After Williams finishes cleaning the car, he joins them in the living room, where Thomas is playing with his barnyard puzzle on the floor, circling the sheep in the air while it waits to be brought down into the only empty space that can hold it. He sits, and there they are on the couch, parents in their twenties, late twenties even, parents but also husband and wife—also husband and wife, Williams thinks—and he wants to remind Adria sometimes that they were husband and wife first, but what for? and what doing? and what doing? and O sweet Williams, what a lucky man you are—I am, thinks Williams—and cheer up now, and smile now please, and she loves you more than him—No, Williams, thinks Williams, not more than, different than—She loves you different than him, and look at your sweet son, and I do love my sweet son, and I know I am lucky, thinks Williams, and I know I am blessed. I am so blessed. And you must wait your turn. You must wait your turn. Because she has had a wonderful turnaround. Postpartum depression free now. Now free. But it is not your turn now. You must wait. Be strong, young man, and he wishes his father had spoken to him that way, and maybe Williams will say to his son one day, Be strong, Young Man, but for today he says to himself in his mind, in his private room, he says, Be strong, Young Man, and he is, and he is because it is a humid Midwest day, and one knows one is alive in the Midwest. Always. Humid or freezing. Humid or freezing. What good is temperance? And he loves the Midwest for more than its green grass and its white snow. He loves it for the large slow mosquitos that arrive with the heat and the small quick ones that leave with it, and the cicadas, and for its ice, the ice that cripples branches, the ice that turns to dirty water in the town's streets. He can barely remember what it was like to live in California, to live without the weather reminding him every few minutes that he has a body.

On the couch, Adria pokes Williams and asks him, "Do you think it's that one guy?"

"I don't know. It could be," he says. "But there are a lot of kids in this neighborhood."

"Sharon thinks he's a gangster. She came by the other day and said to me, 'Do you know you have a gangster walking down your street?'"

"Sharon comes from a town with no stoplights."

"One stoplight."

"What?"

"Her town has one stoplight."

"Is there a difference? Look, Sharon thinks he's a gangster because he's black and where's a blue bandana on his head. That kid's just bored. That's all. He's always walking around listening to his iPod. He's got nothing else to do. And I'm not even sure he did it."

"Then who?"

"I don't know. But I'm not worried. It's not anything personal. It's probably just the car. Maybe the California plates."

"But did it happen to anyone else? You did say you thought some other cars got egged."

"I don't think anyone else got diapered but me. But it would've been a wonderful image."

"What would have?"

"A street full of cars with little cloud-like objects stuck to all the windows."

"You're not taking this seriously enough. What about Thomas?"

"There's nothing to worry about. It happened at night each time, and whoever did it was too scared to go past the street. They didn't touch your car or the house, and they didn't bother to get on the lawn and do the passenger's side."

"So you're not going to do anything?"

"Not yet. A diaper and some honey. There's no use reporting that."

"And the eggs."

"It'll blow over."

"What if it doesn't?"

"It'll blow over."

Most of Williams' time thinking about the composition of his letter occurs when he's driving home from teaching. On weekdays, he would spend anywhere from three to ten hours on campus, depending on whether or not he went to the library to do his own research after teaching. Of course, in the pocket notebook he used to keep track of his time devoted to teaching responsibilities, he didn't include the hours spent reading for and writing his dissertation chapters. That notebook was used only to record the minutes he put into teaching. It's a depressing thing to measure, whether you're a grad student or adjunct instructor, depressing to tally the hourly rate for the full pay of a three unit class. But on a prorated salary? Painful. Foolish. But how elucidating this will be for the dean. How elucidating, thinks Williams, when he tells the dean he earned, what? eight? seven? could it go down to six dollars an hour once the final calculation was in? Williams delights in the absurdity until he remembers his family, their credit card debt, his student loan debt despite a full ride and stipend. It all seems morbidly delicious to Williams until he remembers that he turned down a summer job shelving books at Barnes and Noble as soon as he was the one chosen to teach the only summer fiction class. "Thirty-two hundred dollars," Williams says aloud, driving home in his car in late June. Then he sings it: "Thir-ur-er-ur-ty-two-hu-uhnd-dred-da-a-a-ah-ah-lurs." Instead, he was getting two-hundred a head. Days before he was scheduled to teach, weeks after he turned down the B&N shelf-boy job, they tell him, they, speaking for the dean, they tell him:

—It's up to you, Williams, dear boy. Up to you. The choice is yours not ours. Low enrollment, dear boy. Nothing personal. The *U of M* loves you, and I know you love it too. Go ahead and wear your *M*-hat out, dear boy. Please show some *M*-spirit. But times are tight everywhere. We're not the Ivy Leagues, you know. Times are tight at the *M*s, the *W*s, and the *K*s. Tight at the *I*s too. So the choice is yours. And now I know you wish you'd gotten a dreaded comp class. Those are all full. Thirty-two hundred for your peers suffering through teaching comp. They get full pay for a full class. But you got fiction, lucky boy. You beat out the others craving it too. But oh, eight students only. But cheer up! Two-hundred a head's what we're doing. Two-hundred a head. And there's two days to cheerlead for your class. Two days to recruit. Why fill your class, or just get to ten, and you'll get your thirty-two hundred sweet ones as well, enough to get you through summer. But the comps are all taken. And we've heard that a candidate in philosophy is at the B&N shelving books in your stead, appreciating the order, we suspect, appreciating the alphabetical structure, but you didn't want that job anyway. More income sure, but useless on the cv. You'll choose correctly. And you'll get two hundred a head, sweet one. And try not to lose any of your eight students, sweet doctor-in-training. What's that? We're down to seven students. For shame, only seven on day one. Well, the choice is yours, of course, not ours. Go find another job. I'm sure they're not all taken. Or work for us; you're so talented, by the way. Fourteen hundred's not so bad. Fourteen hundred and one more credit card application. Why not? Just a little more. That chapter on Samuel Menashe you're working on is very necessary. A big contribution to the field. Tenure-track in your future. No adjuncting for you. I see a Research 1 on the horizon. We leave it in your hands. Break the hearts of your seven admirers if you must. But they're worth fourteen hundred now. Now keep them together, you hear. And fill out just one more credit card application. The last one, I suspect, you almost doctor. We're so proud of you, by the way. Your stipend kicks in again with September's gentle arrival. You can make it, sweet one. You're so valuable. Thanks for keeping the class on the books. The seven appreciate it. And so do we—

And Williams recalls these words from the dean's office a month ago, driving home in late June, and he says aloud, "Dear Dean Thurman." And he tries a new opening. "The mood down here is angry. I'm not sure how grad instructors in other departments feel, but we, in the English department, feel taken advantage of. The mood down here is angry." And this leads into his bit about his hourly wage, and he says, "But even so, I wanted you to know that I did a standup job teaching English 163 this summer even though I was paid only $6.82 an hour for my service." Williams spouts off some more and then pulls up to his house and turns off the car. He tells himself to be happy. "Be happy," he says. He wants Adria and Thomas to see him in a good mood when he gets home from the university. "Be happy," he says again, seeing that the summer is vibrant as he walks across his Midwest green lawn and reaches for the doorknob.

After they read Thomas his books and put him to bed, Williams and Adria moved to the kitchen table to unwind with a glass of economy Chablis sprinkled with a little lime soda. A good summertime drink, Adria had told him. The soda helps stretch the bottle. They'd been married for five years, and Williams had never seen Adria dance on a proper stage. It's better this way, she'd told him once. People fall in love with the characters—the elaborate costumes and the makeup—and the atmosphere of a plush theater too. I wouldn't want you to fall for all that.

At the table still, glasses refreshed, Adria takes a sip, then asks, "How'd your class go today?"

They'd spent the first glass talking about parenting. About hypotheticals. Williams is pleased to move on, and so he says, "It was good. It was good, I think."

"What did you do?"

"They'd read a few stories I'd assigned. So we talked about those. We're not in workshop mode yet."

"Anything else?"

Williams almost says, That's about it. Not because he doesn't want to talk to his wife, but because he often doesn't know how to report selectively from topics he can go on and on about, like the structure of the short story or the history of poetic forms in the English language. But they're both good about such things with the other, good about maintaining a genuine interest in the other's art and good—mostly good in Williams' case—about supplying the appropriate amount of information for a layperson, as when Adria discusses Darcy Bussell or that one dancer with the crazy legs—Guillem, is it?

"We talked about characterization," says Willaims. "In the last part of class, I tore out pages from a phonebook and handed them to the students. They had to choose a name and write down all the details they could think of. The easy stuff like appearance and vocation. But also their desires. Their level of contentment. Of course, they're all perfectly happy except for one thing. The characters, that is. Short and plump Billy Niles is trying to get the girl of his dreams. The wealthy and thin William Smarr has a daughter he's trying to reconnect with."

"Were those the names?"

"I don't know. Something like that."

"I want to do it," she says. "You've never told me about this before." She goes to a kitchen drawer and pulls out the most recent phonebook. She sits back down at the table and scoots closer to him, flipping open the white pages to the Ds. "Tell me about Deanna Darrall," she says.

"You tell me." He leans in closer to her and looks down at the page to see the printed name for himself: Darrall Deanna.

"Well, she is a high school English teacher. At Hickly. She likes teaching at the highschool level, not because of the age of the kids—they can really piss her off sometimes—but because she isn't limited by time periods or genres. One day she's teaching Chaucer, the next she's teaching Poe. She loves the sound of her name—Deanna Darrall—even though telemarketers call her and ask for Darrall Deanna, sometimes Mr. Deanna. Her parents are fans of alliteration, of course. They think it's a shame that she must teach *Beowulf* in translation. She likes the falling rhythm of her name. What is it? Trochaic? Dactylic? See, I listen to you. I remember what you tell me."

"I know you do," says Williams.

"She is not lonely, but she would like to find someone. She is the type of teacher who gives out her home number to her students and encourages them to call if they have questions. She has no cats. Oh, but she does go to the bars. She must, right? She goes to the tasteful bars, not the ones with the drunken frat boys, and she orders a vodka martini without olives. If she has not met someone by 8pm, she goes home. She only wants a guy who will approach her before 8pm, you understand. Oh, and the most important details: she's short, she has dark brown hair that reaches her shoulders, her breasts are small, her skin is fair—she's from North Dakota, after all—and she is thirty-seven years old."

Williams leans in and kisses her. And then Adria smiles, and then she says, "That was nice," and then she leans over and kisses him again. The two stay up a bit longer and finish a third drink, and then they go off to bed at the same time, and when she falls asleep, he keeps holding her even though the evening air is warm and her skin is hot.

Days later, in the early evening, Williams is sitting on the couch in their living room, applying online for a new credit card to help defray summer bills. He is trying for a Citi Card because they have two from Chase already loaded down and one from the B of A he just filled up with groceries earlier in the day. He submits his request for a line of two thousand, which would make up the difference in his pay cut since his summer class didn't reach the magic number of ten students. A box pops up on his laptop screen telling him his application will be responded to within a few days.

Adria calls from down the hall. "We're washing hair tonight," she says. "Can you help?"

Williams closes the browser and puts the computer to sleep. "Yes," he says, directing his voice to the open door. He walks into the bathroom and kneels beside his wife. Thomas smiles at him and grabs a blue floating hippo. He shows it to his dad, and then he says, "Hippo."

"Good," says Williams. "Hippo."

Thomas plunges the hippo beneath the water, saying, "Good hippo. Good, good hippo."

Williams shampoos his hair while Adria distracts him with some of the other toys.

"Are you okay?" she asks.

"I'm fine," he says. "It was a long day on campus. I had a lot of reading to get through."

She puts her left hand on his back and keeps it there while he pours cupfuls of water on Thomas's head, angling the cup just so, preventing the suds from streaming to his eyes.

"I might be able to pick up more private lessons," she says.

"That would be good."

"I'll ask around the studio."

"Thanks," says Williams.

They put Thomas to bed together and even sang him songs together, and now Williams walks out to his car to retrieve the groceries he'd left in the back seat that afternoon. When he'd gotten back from the grocery store after his day on campus, he grabbed his book bag and the grocery bags filled with perishables and left the others in the car.

They unpack the remaining groceries together, and Adria turns to Williams and says, "You forgot the ketchup. It's the only way he'll eat his chicken."

"No. It's in there."

"They're all empty," she says, looking annoyed, her eyes big, her brows raised.

Some years ago one of the poems he wrote her had three lines focused on those brows. And he thinks he has known always that he is naïve but he knows it differently now, and he doesn't like this kind of knowing, and he wishes he could still write her lines like those, and he tells himself he will be able to again, and he tells himself he will be able to again, and for now he does not want her to be upset with him, so he asks her gently, "Are you sure?" and then he says right after, "Then the bagger forgot it. Because I know I grabbed it. Look, I'll check the receipt." And he reaches into his pockets, but he can't find it anyway.

"Don't worry," she says. "We'll go back to the store for our morning outing. And then maybe we'll swing by the studio and I'll ask about extra classes."

"Only if you want to," says Williams.

"I do," she says.

Williams appreciates the effort in that "I do" since he is aware that Adria has tired of teaching at the dolly dinkle ballet school where she works on Saturday mornings and occasional afternoons. That's what she calls those small studios with no companies attached to them, dolly dinkles. Five years ago when they chose the Midwest over the East Coast, having decided together that they wanted to get out of California for at least a few years if not forever, Adria had wanted to take a break from the dance world, but she always came back to it. Even after retiring in her twenties, she took on guest spots in companies that sought her out. And places sought her out here as well. Small studios would ask her to dance the lead in their student productions. And she'd do it too. Six months ago she'd danced at an old folks' home with a corps of eight-year-olds surrounding her. The stage was the dining room with the tables pushed against the wall, and the audience was the old folks wheeled out of their rooms for the first part of activity time. Williams stood behind the last row of wheelchairs, holding Thomas, mesmerized by his wife's movements, as he had been when he'd seen her in the few other small productions she'd agreed to. "She's good," one of the old ladies yelled to her neighbor every so often. "She's good." She was San Francisco trained, and Williams saw joy there in his wife as she danced in front of the old folks, joy that had been absent in how she described dancing in San Francisco and elsewhere, retiring in her mid-twenties because of injuries but also and perhaps mostly, Williams had learned, from being tired of bodyness—which is not body image but body form—similar, Williams has thought, to a person being a stanza, a line, a word, a syllable, a phoneme, or perhaps an arm being a unit of structure, a finger another, a glance a fleeting structure, and it is no wonder we borrow bodily terminology to describe our structures—that essay has good bones, that building has good bones, and the dancer is as fluid as writing and she must have good bones but she must have good bone bones and not good metaphor bones, and Williams looks at Adria and he wants to say something profound and he wants them to have the same mind and he wants them to have the same bones, and he swallows, and then he says, "Thanks for taking on some extra work. I appreciate it." And he squeezes her hand gently, and he thinks that maybe he will be able to write her something again sometime soon.

There are a few different routes Williams can take home from the university, and he enjoys varying the drive, sometimes taking the freeway, sometimes taking the streets with the big houses and the old trees canopying the road. But in each case, as he nears his neighborhood, there is only one direct path to his house on Hawthorn Drive, so he always hangs a left on Dogwood Lane after crossing the freeway on Stadium, just as he is doing now, now in the middle of July, which is much warmer than June was, now in the middle of July with all windows down while driving slowly down Dogwood, where duplexes are lined up on a level road, lined up until stopping at the base of a slight hill where single-family homes begin. He had taken a slow drive home from campus, passing through a neighborhood nicknamed "professorville," where many of the roads were still red brick and where "Notable Historic Property" signs were placed in front yards. But now Williams is driving carefully on Dogwood, because children often played in the front yards of this sidewalkless and somewhat busy street, where most of the lawns are mowed even though the grass sprouts up quickly with the summer rains, where most of the duplexes are rentals yet taken care of with a look of pride one might mistake for pride of ownership, and Williams' left arm is propped up on the door, and his shirt cuff is angled in such a way that air streams in at his wrist and flows up his arm. And the kid whom his wife's friend had called a gangster is walking on the left side of the street. He is walking toward Williams and his slowly-moving Lincoln, and after Williams passes him he looks into his rearview mirror and sees the kid throw his arms up at him. Williams hits the brakes and does a three-point turn in the middle of the road. He parks hastily along the curb and hops out of the car. The kid stands there waiting for him, arms still raised.

"Don't do that," Williams says.

"Come and get this!" says the kid.

Williams walks up to him with his arms stretched out in front of his body and his fingertips pointed upward. "We need to talk," says Williams.

The kid lowers his arms. "What do you want?"

"You can't do that to me. You can't raise your hands up like that when I drive by."

"You're driving around here like you're all bad," the kid says.

"I'm not bad," says Williams. "I'm not driving around here trying to be tough. I'm just getting home. You know where I live, right?"

The kid nods. "I see your car parked up there. When I'm walking to the park."

"That's right," says Williams. "And I drive by your house every day. I go to work. I go to the grocery store. I just drive by. I see you sitting on your porch. I see you walking up and down the street. And you see me driving by. Every day. Driving right by you."

"So what."

"We're neighbors. That's all. I'm not trying to get a rise out of you when I drive by. I know I look over at you. That's just what I do. I notice people. I look at them. I'm not trying to get a rise out of you."

"Then stop acting so tough, man. Stop cruising with that pompous look."

"I'm not tough," Williams says. "I'm not cruising. I'm just driving. Come here. I want to show you something."

The kid doesn't move.

"I don't want to fight you," says Williams. "I'm a nice guy. And you are too. I just want to show you my car."

"I can see it," says the kid.

"What's your name?" asks Williams.

"Arthur."

"Arthur, I'm Williams. I'll wave to you the next time I drive by and you're walking down the street. Okay. But I'd like to show you this car."

Arthur walks over to where Williams is standing. Williams opens the passenger door. "Get in for a second."

"I'm not getting in there."

"Keep the door open if you want. Just sit down, please. I want to show you something."

Arthur sits in the passenger seat and keeps the door open. Williams walks around to the other side and gets into the driver's seat.

"So what," Arthur says.

"Take a look at this," says Williams. "It's a chess piece. A rook."

"I know what it is."

"It's my favorite piece. I keep it there as a reminder of when I used to play."

"What the hell are those?"

"Pipe holders," says Williams. "This was my grandfather's car. He gave it to me when he died. He was a preacher in Ohio, and he would often go on these long road trips. See he smoked a pipe. But he didn't like to have to stop driving to pack a new one. So he began a drive with two packed up to the brim, and when one was smoked up he'd set it down and light the other. Then at gas stops he'd repack them both and keep going."

"Do you smoke a pipe?"

"I tried, but I couldn't keep it lit. I'd have to keep relighting it after a few puffs. It was too much work." The pair is silent for a few seconds. "So anyway," Williams goes on. "When you see me drive by, I want you to think of this rook sitting here. I want you to think of these pipe holders on the dash, the rook in the one and the stamps and paperclips in the other. I want you to think, there goes that fool who tried to smoke a pipe and couldn't keep the damn thing lit."

The humidity in July rose steadily as the month came to a close. Heat indices stayed above 100 degrees, and Williams hadn't seen Arthur walking around since their encounter some days back. On Friday, July 30 Williams collected and graded his students' final portfolios, and then he checked his and Adria's account that evening and saw that the second $658 had been deposited. Unlike four weeks earlier, he had no hope that his full paycheck might have been awarded to him.

On the next morning, Williams has the air conditioning running as he drives to the downtown post office to mail his letter to the dean. The letter is two pages single-spaced. He had written it in a single sitting at the beginning of the week, and then he worked on it for a few hours each day, cutting its content in half and adding and rearranging elements until every sentence was sharp. He is proud of the letter. It is filled with logic and emotion, and its personal bias does not cloud its persuasiveness. He wrote eloquently and tersely, and he was careful to avoid an unnecessary rant on the validity of creative writing courses. It was not the course that was being questioned, he had reminded himself. It was the unwillingness to pay him a full wage to guide seven students into earning three more units toward their degrees. What would have changed at ten students, or even the full fifteen? Williams had asked in the finished letter.

Williams enters the drive-through line for the outside mailboxes. There are no cars behind him, and the two cars ahead of him finish up and he now pulls alongside one of the blue boxes. He takes a first-class forever stamp from the right-side pipe holder and places it on the envelope. The letter is addressed to the dean's office, just a few hundred yards south of there. Williams wants his letter to get to the dean as quickly as possible. He is wondering if he should use intercampus mail instead. Perhaps now he should just drive down there and deliver it personally, he thinks. But surely the office is locked on Saturday, and the only keys he has are to the English department in Krekly Hall. He stares at the envelope. "Dean Alexander Thurman" is the first line in the center, but now he worries about the second line—"The Office of the Dean"—written in slightly smaller letters beneath the name. Would the letter ever get to the dean? Williams wonders. Would a lower-down read it and then summarize it in a brief meeting. Nothing to worry about, the lower-down would tell the dean. Just someone who's a little upset. Nothing wrong on our end.

Williams can't let that happen. He sets the letter on the passenger's seat, and then he looks in his rearview mirror. No one is there. He keeps his foot on the brake and reaches back with his right hand, searching the backseat floor for his characterization-day phonebook. He feels a heavy plastic bottle and brings it to the front seat. The missing ketchup. Williams tosses it onto the passenger's side floor and reaches into the backseat again, this time emerging frontward with the weighty phonebook. He flips to Thurman. There is a dozen of them, but no Alexanders. "Thurman A" is the only possibility. Williams flips through the book some more to see how many people he knows are listed. The gaps from the pages he'd torn out prevent him from checking some of them, but he discovers that most of the people he can think of are all there. He had even searched for his own professors, and most of them were listed too. And now he flips to the Cs, not remembering if he and Adria had chosen to be in there. He is, but she isn't. "Craig Williams," and then the phone number but not the address—the phone number that telemarketers would call to speak with a Mr. Williams. Am I speaking with Craig? one would ask. Do I have Mr. Williams on the line? another would say. You've got Williams, Williams would respond. You've got Mr. Craig, he would say if they still didn't get it.

Williams flips back to "Thurman A." He knows the address. He checks his mirror again. His is still the only car in the mailbox line. Then he pulls forward and drives out of downtown, heading west on Lincoln into a neighborhood adjacent to the university. A. Thurman's street is quiet for a Saturday morning. The skies are clear, but there are no children in sight. Williams pulls up to the curb across the street from A. Thurman's house.

He turns off the engine and sits there with the windows down. The house is magnificent, but it isn't excessive, not over-the-top, Williams thinks. It's respectable. Each home on the street is respectable—two stories, mostly brick, most with flowers in planters and all with full trees. There's nothing pretentious about them, though they are some of the older homes in the city. Williams grabs the letter off the passenger's seat and walks across the street. There is one car in the driveway in front of the Thurman's garage. Other homes have cars parked in the driveways too, but there are few cars parked along the curbs, hardly any cars on the street compared to the number of houses, just large shady trees in front of spaced-out properties. He stands at the front door holding the letter. The envelope and the two pages within it are light in his hand, but everything is in there. He had condensed it all. The weight of his twenty-nine years is behind it. The final figure turned out to be $7.52 an hour. It could have been less. It can always be less. He could have written longer comments on their works and he could have spent more time planning the so-called lecture days instead of occasionally winging them. But what does it matter? He got the job done, and he suspects he did it well enough to get decent evaluations. He puts the letter in the mailbox by the door and then returns to his car.

He turns the engine on and sits there for a minute. The street is still empty. He checks his rearview mirror to pull out safely, and then he catches sight of the parking permit hooked to the mirror, realizing that he had forgotten to deduct the permit's cost in his final figure. Damn it, Williams thinks. He'd purchased the summer permit for just over $100, not too big of a sacrifice to make for the full three-unit salary, but for the seven-head pre-tax $1400 it is outrageous. Williams keeps the car running and hops out to retrieve the letter. The mailbox lid squeaks when it didn't earlier, but no one inside seems to stir and Williams darts back to his car without confrontation. He holds the envelope, unsure of what to do. He could go home and print out a new copy with the updated wage, but that seems ridiculous to him now. The letter would be received the same. Williams knows that. He could have fabricated the figure and typed up any number. In the end, it isn't the exact hourly wage that matters. He might as well put this version back. But he doesn't. He sees himself in the rearview mirror. He looks pathetic. You are pathetic, he thinks. He pulls off the permit and examines the thin plastic that usually went unnoticed, the thin plastic that is too great an embodiment of his summer earnings. The plastic as thick as the one-month-old Citi Card tucked into his wallet.

Williams keeps the car running as he sits there holding the letter and the permit, and then he tosses them both to the passenger's side floor. The permit clacks against the ketchup bottle before landing on the floor mat. Williams picks up the ketchup and exits the running car. He moves quickly to the Thurmans' driveway and pauses at the car's trunk. It is a modest green car with a small trunk. Williams is sure the dean's car must be in the garage, so this one will have to do. It probably belongs to one of his kids. And does he have kids? Williams wonders. Of course, he does. He must. And his daughter or his son will rise shortly and read this message, and then the dean will be gathered to read the message. So Williams now walks around to the hood, where he'll have a bit more writing space. He aims the bottle near the center and squirts hard. But nothing happens. He twists off the cap and then removes the pull-away factory tab. He puts the cap back on and tries again, this time directing the thick liquid into even block letters: YOU SHOULD HAVE JUST CANCELED IT. He stares at the sentence, embarrassed by the unnecessary adverb. He thinks for a second—unconcerned by the house facing his back, its windows above the garage or their curtains that might be cracking right then, and unconcerned by the neighbors' windows too— and then he puts a ketchup line through the "just" and rewrites the clause again, directly beneath the first one, adding a "for me" to its end and a "because I never could have" beneath that. He looks at his work:

YOU SHOULD HAVE ~~JUST~~ CANCELED IT.
YOU SHOULD HAVE CANCELED IT FOR ME
BECAUSE I NEVER COULD HAVE.

This is good, Williams thinks, but he knows something is missing. He stands a moment longer, and then it hits him, and he supplies the missing content, scoring the whole space of the hood:

DEAR DEAN THURMAN,
YOU SHOULD HAVE ~~JUST~~ CANCELED IT.
YOU SHOULD HAVE CANCELED IT FOR ME
BECAUSE I NEVER COULD HAVE.
SINCERELY,
ONE OF THE UNDERVALUED

Williams darts back to the running car, sets the ketchup bottle on the passenger's seat, and drives down the street, not looking back at the house, driving slowly like someone who's under control. There are no sirens. There are no watchful Thurmans or neighbors yelling after him, running to keep pace with his old Lincoln.

The image of the lettered hood is burned into Williams' mind. He sees it on the road as he heads home. The big red letters filling up the small green hood remind him of Christmas. He sees the letters etched in the tar road and gripping the sky, and the sky is gray in the distance ahead of him, and he doesn't know if that is the sky's real color right now or if he wants a storm cloud to come and wash over the hood, and he thinks that maybe that color is blue, and he thinks that maybe the sky is always without color and he is always filling it in, and he wants to be that needed by everybody without anybody knowing it, and he wants the color of the sky to be partly made by him, and he is thinking these things when he turns down Dogwood, when he sees Arthur walking toward him on the other side of the street, and Williams waves to him, and Arthur offers a kind of half wave, and Williams is just glad he didn't throw his arms up. That's all that matters, Williams thinks. He parks along the curb in front of his house and turns off the engine. He picks up the letter on the floor, and carefully with his nails he peels off the stamp and sticks it back on the roll he keeps in the right pipe holder. He sets the letter back on the floor and walks up to his house. He sees Adria and Thomas through the living room window. Thomas waves to him, and he waves back, pressing his fingertips to his palm, again and again, repeating the motion, waving like a child, unaware that he is doing so.

café

They are sitting at a café. This is a story about him and her. That's all you need. Him and her. But what can happen to him and her? They are not sitting at just any café. They are sitting in a Denny's on 7th Street. It is 4am. Did they arrive together? They did, yes. Are they early risers, or did they come to the Denny's after a late night out together? The latter's expected, so these two—this pair sitting in the glow of Denny's 4am light, this pair divided on two slick booth seats—got out of bed together, dressed near each other, drove there together, and now they are here, Denny's cream-colored mugs with brown rims on the tabletop, different shades of coffee in each mug, a similar steam from the fresh pour rising, his hands encircling one mug, her hands out of view, and from this side view their faces are not quite visible. Only they can see their faces. We will not see them this time, and when the pair first came into side focus and when the tabletop that must link or separate took shape between them, I was going to tell you that we don't know why they got up so early, and I was going to tell you that all we know is that one of them will leave the other. Him or her. I was going to say that I would like to tell you otherwise. I was going to say that the only thing I've known since *They are sitting* is that one is going to leave the other while the air stays crisp outside and can be nothing other than crisp outside while they are inside, in some café. And I am wanting to write *But look now, sweet reader,* but instead I write *But look now, sweet writer,* and so I look, and her hands rise from beneath the tabletop, brought forth from her lap, and they settle on the clean surface between them.

some substantial thing

I t was nearly midnight when she entered the bar to meet her friend. He had something to tell her, something that needed to be disclosed in person, so she had agreed to a late-night meeting even though she was studying in her apartment, even though she disliked bars in the evening and did not need to be pulled away from her heavily scored paperback of Christina Rossetti's *Complete Poems*. The outside air was crisp, and she had walked quickly from her apartment, the collar of her pea coat turned up against the winter. She arrived first, and even though the bar was filled with people conversing, she managed to find an empty table with two chairs along the back wall. She sat and began to wait for her friend, and a waitress approached her and she ordered a vodka cranberry, and the waitress returned with it as if no time had passed, and this college-aged girl twirled her straw around the ice in her drink, wondering what her friend needed to talk to her about.

The muffled sound of engaged voices occupied the air, and if there was music playing, she could not hear it above the chatter. The light was dim but bright enough, and this bar seemed to be just about the same as the few others she'd been in, all of which had been close to campus and walking distance to her apartment, her apartment just like any bookish student's apartment in a small downtown in a Midwest college town that is a midsized city, a studio filled with novels and poetry collections and the vanishing air of hopeful conversations, conversations like many of those around her, and she had been sitting for a minute or two inside this bar before she realized that she could make out the discussion of the two men at the table nearest her.

She directed her left ear toward the pair while studying the redness of her drink so as to be discreet, hearing one of them say, "I have a friend who has a similar theory about interpretation."

She glanced at him before returning her eyes to the tabletop, and she recognized him as a professor in her department, in his mid-thirties and oddly handsome, or charming somehow, or perhaps she just had that impression now from the quick glimpse of his green or blue sweater vest because she did recall him having a really crooked nose when she'd seen him before in Tate Hall.

And then this professor sipped his drink, and then he continued his thought, and she listened in and let his words fill her mind as she stared at the blankness of her glossy tabletop.

"He hadn't read anyone," the professor said to his companion. "He admitted this, this friend of mine. I haven't read anyone, he'd said. And I don't speak your jargon. But he went on. He went on and said that he always marveled at graffiti artists covering up each other's works. And no-talents spraying simple words and names over their works. The talented and untalented each covering up what someone has done before. He saw me think that I had made his connection. My fat face must have glowed the way we do when we are proud of discovering something. But he saw me glowing and he dragged it out. Took a sip and then another. No, he said. Not that. And he went on to say that it's how you look at a work, how a viewer covers up the work. Not the whole thing. But covers sections of it. I get this part here, he said. Gesturing to an imagined corner. I like it. We'll leave this corner alone. It's a good one. But this. Gesturing above. I don't get this. I will make sense of this. I will write my mind can all over this."

His friend interjected, "He said mind-can?"

She looked over at the second man. His wispy hair was thinning near his forehead, but his skin looked tight and she guessed he was in his late twenties, six years or so older than she was. She had never seen him before in her department or around campus, but she suspected that he too was an academic of some sort, whether a graduate student or young professor.

"Yes, he said mind-can," said the professor in the sweater vest, "but he's a good guy, really. And somewhat bright. Don't dwell on that. So where was I?" A waitress then approached the men and said something, and this slightly older one responded, "Excuse me? Yes, that will be fine. The same for each. More croc in the crocodile. My wife says that. She got it from Angela Lansbury, she says. She has funny tastes. Bless her."

The waitress looked over at the girl's still-full drink and then turned to walk back to the bar, and the girl kept listening as the younger man answered his colleague's question from before the waitress's interruption, saying, "I think you'd gotten to the point. That viewers' interpretations write over the parts of a painting they feel uncomfortable with."

"Yes, true," said the professor in the sweater vest, "nothing new there, but get this. Hear what this friend of mine did. So he finds this wall. This big empty wall. It's in that shopping district west of downtown. With the trendy stores. So this big brick wall painted entirely white. A side of an outdoorsy store. And at midnight or so he sets up with flood lights and cones and ladders. And caution signs and makes the whole thing look professional. And he paints all night long. And it all looks official. A cop came by I think. Stood and watched him work for a while before walking on. Never asked for a permit."

"I get it," said the younger one.

The professor she recognized held up his hand to his younger colleague and then kept talking. "So he finishes up and leaves before it's light. And what did he paint, you wonder? That's just it. It's awful." The waitress returned to their table, holding a tray with two amber-colored drinks with no ice, and the professor said, "Oh good, yes here's room." And then he picked up his old glass and said, "Wait, one more sip." And then he finished the last of his old drink and handed her the empty glass, and he said, "Okay, that one too. Good. Thank you." And she grabbed his friend's empty glass also, set down the two new drinks, and walked away, and the professor in the sweater vest continued talking to his slightly younger colleague, saying, "So it's a big serene lake with two kayakers pleasantly stroking along, and there's the sun setting or rising, and there are trees, maybe a moose or something sipping the lake somewhere. It's that scene, you know."

"So he gave the store a free mural," said the younger one, sipping amber from his new glass. "So what?"

"No," said the older one, "I mean yes, he did, but they get screwed over. It wasn't a nice thing. And he knew it, and he felt bad for them, but he wanted to prove a point. He set up a video camera across the street in his loft. Did I tell you that he lived across the street?"

"No."

"Well, he did. He does. He lives across the street in this apartment loft thing, and the once-white brick wall was down below one of his windows. So he had a camera pointed at this kayak mural thing, and it kept recording onto his computer."

"I'm getting tired," said the one with wispy hair and tighter cheek skin.

"We're almost there. Here, sip with me. And so what happens?"

"He watches and sees whether or not people like the thing."

"What? No, of course not. He waits for people to tag it. Don't you remember where we started? *Il faut vous enivrer.* He had a theory that involved graffiti artists."

The girl didn't know French, and she felt left out and embarrassed for her eavesdropping self.

"I remember now," said the younger one. "I'm just tired. *Sans trêve.* You missed part of the line. *Sans trêve.*"

"It's not a line," the older one said.

"True," said the younger one.

And the girl figured out that they had recited part of a French prose poem, and even though she did not know why, she was pleased with herself for getting that much, and in her joy it occurred to her to take a sip of her now watered down cranberry vodka, and it tasted pungent to her even though diluted, so she stirred her straw around some more and kept listening in.

The professor in the sweater vest sipped again, and then he asked his colleague friend, "You teach in the morning?"

"Ten."

"Okay, sleep soon, but hear this," the older one went on. "So he recorded the wall for weeks, months, I think. And it went through all these transformations. And at night there is a soft light from a streetlight, so you can see the taggers approach the wall. And some spray really beautiful little pictures. Others really decorative script. Some crude block lettering. The unskilled who think they should be joining in. And you see bits of the awful mural get covered over, but some things stay untouched. No one dared spray over the moose head. But the lake got it. And the people? Forget about it. And of course, some tags got covered over by other tags. And eventually, this messy multi-author thing was up there."

"And?"

"Well, the store owners, they decided to repaint the brick wall white.

They had liked the mural at first. My friend had overheard someone say that they'd been pleasantly surprised that morning. But it grew ugly to them. So it became white again. And do you know what? No one has touched it since. It's been weeks. The thing is all white still."

"I'm going to bed," said the younger one.

"But you see why I told you this?"

"Yes. But it's not the same. My piece is more complicated. I didn't explain it right. You'll see. Read it when it comes out. A few weeks away I think. Read it when it comes out. I do something different. You'll see. I didn't quite explain it well enough, I suppose."

"No, of course not. You did a fine job. Entirely different. I misspoke. And different media anyway. Different by definition anyway. You get some sleep. We'll talk about other things tomorrow. There're always other things. I'm keeping you. Yes, please, off to bed."

The young colleagues shook hands, and the wispy-haired one stood and then walked away after placing a bill on the table, and the professor she recognized from her department cupped both hands around his glass, leaned back in his chair, and seemed to take notice of a conversation going on at another table near his, and his crooked yet distinguished nose nodded slowly and slightly at what he heard, and the eavesdropping girl realized that her hands were cold from cupping her own glass, and she remembered that she was sitting there alone and that she was waiting for her dear friend to meet her and tell her some substantial thing, and she wished he was there now, she wished that he had not taken so long, and she wished him into being there because then she saw him walking in, looking for her, and she sprang to her feet, abandoning her table and her drink, bumping past the now-alone-sitting-sweater-vested professor with odd charm, and she crooked her arm into her friend's arm as he stood near the door, and she pulled him outside with her, and the linked duo shuffled down the icy sidewalk, and her friend had not yet said a word, his crinkling face painting surprise on his normally collected face, a face framed by a dark hat and a dark scarf, and they were roughly the same height and build as she led them to a streetlight with an orange glow illuminating the naked arms of wintry trees, and then she stopped, and then they looked at each other, and she said to him, "I don't know if you love me or someone else, but I know that you love someone, and I want it to be me, and I want you to say something to me now as if it is exactly what you would have said to me before I said this, and it will be exactly what you would have said, okay, and now you'll say something and I'll stop talking, but first I am going to kiss you," and she kissed him on the lips with perfect inexperience, and he kissed her back as clumsily, and they separated, and she looked at him, and he looked at her, and she felt the impulse to talk because she could control her words, but she waited now as she had been waiting, and the air stayed cold, and he would say something soon about one thing or another.

into the ends of the world

In a crowd of twenty or so Alan stood at the bus stop on a February
morning in what had been an unusually cold winter for Oakland.
People didn't look at home bundled in scarves and gloves and thicker
jackets than normal. But the good thing was that maybe it pulled people
together a bit more, since here was a group of strangers standing close and
chatting before they were forced to be near one another on the bus. Back in
the fall, before the chill set in, this same group would be spread out along
the curb before the bus pulled up to corral them together. The 82-line down
International Boulevard took most people to work this early in the morning,
but Alan was heading to his internship at North County Jail, and today he
would say goodbye to Craig before he was shipped up to San Quentin and
put on death row.

Everyone had a closed umbrella. Alan's stretched out across the top of
his worn leather satchel, strapped to the top near the handles. His breathing
and everyone's breathing created wisps that shot out and drifted up before
disintegrating. Visible puffs born from nostrils and mouths. Going out and
up. Out and up. A few blocks down the street the 82 neared. The people
closest to the curb craned their necks, the bus's square front having been
located through the grayness. And the crowd groaned and muttered "finally"
together, but when the bus was on their block, it kept going past, and the bus
driver had looked over at the crowd for a brief moment and then straight
ahead again as he kept up his speed, the bus's windows revealing torsos and

arms crammed together. In the wake of the full bus, leaves and debris whirled up, then settled back down to the pavement, and everyone started another round of waiting.

After what felt to Alan like five minutes of waiting, another 82 bus showed up, and it had enough room for this crowd to board, enough room for each person, one at a time, to climb the steep grooved stairs. Inside, Alan stood in the back, gripping the metal bar running parallel to the ceiling. The bus bounced along International Boulevard, and Alan and the other standers used hands, limbs, and stances to stay upright throughout each stop and start and stop and start, throughout the increasing crowding that wouldn't let up until the bus reached downtown. No one was really looking at Alan, who had a thick black beard he'd grown in the last few months and thick black hair on his head slicked straight back. He wasn't trying to look intimidating, and he didn't think he looked intimidating since he was a regular smiler at people, but ever since he started doing visitations in the jail he wanted to blend in a bit more with the men he was helping. They didn't all have beards, of course, but Alan had a thin face and was only nineteen, so since he was able to grow a full beard, he went ahead and did it, and in a way it helped him be a stronger, surer version of himself in the moments he held hands to pray with men who had killed others, men who often made him want to reach out and strangle them for all those they hurt.

But he was always composed on the outside. Always composed. And there were many inmates he'd developed a fondness for, men he'd sympathize for despite their actions, men like Craig, whom he'd visited frequently ever since starting the internship. His trial had been all over the papers, a twice-convicted burglar who held a job as a house painter. He was the last known person to be at a murder scene—a house whose interior and exterior he'd painted—a three day job, and he said he finished around 1pm on the last day, and later that afternoon the mother and child were found dead in the living room, and things were missing, stolen, so it seemed to be an easy conviction for the jurors despite the lack of violence in Craig's past, despite the lack of evidence—no recovered stolen items—and despite Chaplain Castillo's heavy involvement in the case, testifying in court in favor of Craig's character, doing interviews with reporters, and inserting himself in the corner of the accused in a way he had never done before in his twenty-five years as chaplain.

The bus kept its stop and go journey toward downtown, and Alan kept clenching and releasing his right forearm muscles each time a wheel hit a bump. To his left a woman sat reading the city section of the *Tribune*. He'd read it that morning, as he did every morning, to follow the cases of the more high-profile inmates he visited. The page she was reading had a new article on Hector Ruiz, who six months ago murdered his girlfriend and her lover by barricading them in her Berkeley home and setting it on fire. When Alan had visited him a few days after he'd been arrested, he brought Hector the Bible he'd requested, and Hector held the thick paperback above his head and said that he'd been lost without it, without his sword and shield.

Eventually, the bus crossed over the East Oakland barrier into downtown. And at the next stop, when the bus was still two stops from the jail, a former inmate named Junebug climbed up the steps, mumbled something to the driver, and searched his hands in his pockets until he found a bus transfer. The driver took the thin paper without seeming to look at the time or even the date. Junebug had been in and out of the jail in the months that Alan had been interning. Always for a minor charge of vagrancy or drug possession. He'd put in some time and then get back out only to get back in within a week or two. He was a fixture at the jail, what they called a revolving door inmate. As he started down the aisle to sit or stand somewhere, Junebug saw Alan and smiled widely. This happened every once in a while, running into a former inmate out in the street, or on the bus.

Junebug sauntered up to Alan, reaching out a hand before he was close enough for Alan to take it. "Young chaplain," said Junebug. "Oh, it's good to see you. How's it going? You off to work? Heading to the building?"

Alan accepted his hand and gave it a quick shake. The hand was warm and damp. Junebug reeked of sweat and whiskey. But the whiskey was mild compared to the smell of unwashed skin and heavy clothes, to the smell of dried sweat mingling with the new sweat dripping on the old stuff, like the beads on his forehead that were probably from running down the street to catch this bus in time. "It's good to see you too, Junebug," said Alan. "It's good to see you here, on this bus."

"That's true," said Junebug. "It's good to be here together. Instead of the resort. Instead of on vacation."

Alan looked out of the window to see if the next stop was close. He pulled down the cord running above the windows on his side, and the STOP REQUESTED light shone at the bus's front. Former inmates often used the word vacation to refer back to a completed prison sentence, and they don't use it lightheartedly, and they don't use it to refer back to quick stints in and out of jail. There was an old timer in Alan's church who served ten years for bad decisions, as he'd said, and when he was a gap in someone's story or when he'd talk about not being around for something, he'd say—That's when I was on vacation, or, I was on vacation then—and there was regret in his voice, and vacation meant—I'm not going back—and vacation meant—I went a long time missing birthdays and anniversaries and graduations, but it was a one-time deal. Just a one-time deal.

"Junebug," Alan said. "My internship is ending soon. I won't be the chaplain's assistant much longer."

"I'm sorry," said Junebug.

"No, it's fine. I mean, it's supposed to end." The bus slowed. "But I just wanted to say," said Alan, "I just want to say that you should try not to go back. You should not go back at all, I mean."

"I don't plan on it." The bus stopped and Alan leaned toward the back door. "I certainly don't plan on that," said Junebug. "So you take care. You're a real help to everyone. A better listener than the old chaplain. He goes on and on."

"Thanks," said Alan. "And don't take this the wrong way, but I hope I don't see you again. Unless it's on this bus, of course. But I don't want to see you again in the next few weeks in there. Do that for me as a going away present." The bus's back door folded inward and opened up by itself, and Alan stepped down. "But if you're in there, I'll see you," he said. "But try not to be."

Outside, Alan walked two blocks to the jail since he'd gotten off the bus a stop early. The jail stretched up into the downtown sky, which was part blue but mostly gray still. The jail was eight stories high not counting the ground floor, but each story had to have been around twenty feet since it contained two levels of cells. The windows were tall and thin, maybe a couple feet high but only a few inches wide. Stacks of sixteen at each corner of the building. When Alan had started his internship and was still set on the idea of becoming a prison chaplain one day, he would stare at the outside of the building after a day of maneuvering inside, and he would map out on the wall the different levels he'd visited, trying to match windows with inmates, at least those who were allowed to have one. The jail had been built on giant springs. It could withstand an eight-point earthquake, Alan was told, and he sometimes remembered that fact when he'd walk up to it, and he'd picture it bobbing back and forth like a big jack-in-the-box, this imposing structure bending but not breaking when other buildings were crumbling, this imposing structure left as the only thing standing in downtown Oakland after some disaster, its occupants held safely within.

In the ground floor of the jail, Alan walked toward the service window, passing rows of connected chairs filled with people waiting for visiting hours. At the service window, two women sat comfortably behind an inch of bulletproof glass. Alan took out his driver's license from his wallet and slid it into the groove beneath the glass.

"Good morning, Jean," he said.

"Morning," she said, exchanging his license for his county ID badge.

She printed his name and entrance time on the sign-in sheet and slid it beneath the glass for him to sign. He scribbled his signature, and Jean put his license in one of the small cubbies behind the counter.

"Do you need a deputy?" she asked. "Or are you just going up to the offices?"

"Just the offices for now," he said. "Thanks."

"Sure, hon," she said.

She pushed a button, and the large door on the west side of the counter buzzed open. Alan walked through the open door and into a small area with two other doors. He stared up at the camera on the ceiling, and he felt guilty of something—or accused of something maybe—each time he looked at a camera in this building. The door closed behind him, and after the clicking of metal locks, another door opened, this one leading to the administrative offices, which were adjacent to but separate from the jail. He walked through this second door and up to an elevator, pushing its button, stepping inside, and traveling up to the fourth floor, where he walked down a corridor of shut doors before walking into the chaplain's open office.

The chaplain sat at his desk with his back to the door. Alan set down his bag and umbrella by the wall, and the chaplain turned to him and said, in an even voice, "You're fifteen minutes late."

Alan knew he was trying to be stern, but the chaplain couldn't keep it up because he started laughing as Alan answered, "So was my bus."

"No, no, it's fine," said the chaplain. "I'm kidding, of course. How are you? Lots to do today. Did you bring your paper?"

"I'm good, thanks. Have the paper in my bag." The chaplain had often assigned Alan essays to write as part of his internship even though he wasn't getting course credit. "I saw Junebug on the bus a few minutes ago."

"That guy. How did he look?"

"All right, I suppose. Pretty put together."

"He'll be back in here soon."

"I know. That's the thing. I told him not to come back. I said, Make sure you stay out of here. But I never know what to say when I see them on the outside. It doesn't happen much. But I feel like I need to say something. I know what to say in here. I'm getting that down."

"You really are. You're doing well."

"But what can I say to a guy like Junebug outside?"

"There's not much. You did fine. It's bigger than you. So you can't worry about it. That's part of the problem, isn't it? There are some guys putting in long time who should be out already, and there are those who pop in and out so often they should just never leave. Junebug is Junebug. He probably won't ever change. Not without a time machine anyway. Not without undoing a lot of things you can't fix now."

Alan took off his coat and put it on the back of the desk chair in the corner. The chaplain had the desk and chair brought in seven months ago. Alan knew he enjoyed the extra company. There were some other volunteers who had been cleared to do visitations, but even the regular ones came once or twice a week at most, so on an average Monday through Friday, it was just the chaplain and Alan filling book orders and visitation requests. The corner desk had a pile of inmate request forms on it.

"Try and get through all those," the chaplain said. "I'm going to start my rounds."

"Of course," said Alan.

"I'll come back for lunch, and afterward, we'll get you on the floors."

"Sounds good." Alan grabbed the stack of requests and sat down, and then he asked, "Have you seen Craig yet?"

"For an hour this morning. Around six. It was good. We prayed together. We kept it light. I've told the chaplain at San Quentin about him. Gary's his name. Nice guy."

"That's good," said Alan. "I'm glad he's handling it all right."

"He is. Better than most. But that's because he's got the Lord. He's going to do good things over there. He's going to be a light out there. I still can't believe those dumbshits convicted him. That I'll never understand. But he's dealing with it. He's come to peace with it." The chaplain stepped out of his office door but then turned back to face Alan. "Don't worry. You'll get to see him today. I know you two are close. I'll make sure you get to say goodbye."

The chaplain had violated one of his own rules by getting so involved in Craig's case. When he was training Alan before allowing him on the jail floors to meet with inmates, the chaplain told him not to talk to them about their cases. A lot of them will only want to talk to you about their cases, he'd said. They'll request visitations thinking that you can help them with their case. But you can't do that, said the chaplain. You can't help them in that way, so brush it off when they bring it up. Move off that topic and on to something else.

Alone in the office Alan sifted through the request slips, separating them into three piles, one for books only, one for visitations only, and one for both books and visitations. Out of the more than eight hundred inmates, about fifty would complete a form each day. And the ones that the chaplain or Alan or the occasional volunteer could not get to that day would be put at the top of the pile for the next day. The inmates requested Bibles, Korans, and even the occasional Book of Mormon, and they requested devotional readings and really whatever they could get their hands on. The chaplain's office was full of large bookcases loaded down with paperback Bibles and other texts. Most of them came out of his budget, but occasionally they received a box of books donated from some religious press. For the request slips asking for books or books and a visit, Alan would comb through the shelves and do his best to accommodate them, usually limiting each inmate to two to three books, as he'd been advised. He would then stamp the request slip COMPLETED and write the date down and sign it, and then he would rubberband the books together and place a post-it note on top, writing the inmate's name, number, and floor/block/cell location. As he created stacks of books to be delivered, he would place them in boxes grouped by floors. The work was tedious, but Alan knew it was important, so he didn't mind. Occasionally the request slips would ask for him personally. Inmates sometimes wrote, *I'd like to see the young chaplain* or *Can I please talk with the new chaplain*, and once he was referred to as the *chaplain in training* since he always corrected anyone who called him a chaplain by mistake, not because he liked correcting people but because he knew he hadn't earned that title yet.

After three hours of Craig organizing visitation requests and filling four boxes with book requests, the chaplain returned from doing his visitations and the two went to the employee cafeteria for an early lunch. The cafeteria was filled mostly with deputies, but there was the occasional table of clerical workers who never stepped foot into the jail side. The chaplain and Alan sat at a table by themselves, as they usually did. The lunch today was grilled chicken, mashed potatoes, and peas. Alan didn't think the food there was too bad.

The two ate without much conversation after they had put their trays down and the chaplain prayed for their meal. The cafeteria was noisy all the time. It was crowded now, but even in off hours there was usually at least one table full of deputies talking loudly, enjoying each other's company after long shifts of little talking and having their defenses up, sitting behind dark glass and watching and watching, or moving inmates here and there and cuffing them and uncuffing them, cuffing and uncuffing and always alert, always on guard. But in here they were loud talkers and easygoing and liked being around each other. And there were crowded tables all around the chaplain and Alan's mostly empty table, and then the chaplain looked up at Alan and, after chewing and swallowing, said, "And what is your paper titled? The paper due today."

"The Detriment of Incarceration," said Alan.

"Careful," whispered the chaplain, looking from side to side. "You know they see us as a big enough nuisance as it is."

Early on in his internship Alan once made the mistake of referring to a deputy as a guard. The deputy looked at him coldly after he said it, and then later in the day when that deputy was supposed to retrieve him from a multipurpose room after a visit with an inmate, the deputy left him in there for two hours before getting him, saying that there was a situation with the inmate he was putting back that held him up. The chaplain later explained that only prisons have hired guards. Jails use deputies, he'd said. Don't forget that we're a jail, not a prison. They don't like being called guards, he'd said. You'll need to remember that.

And now the chaplain asked, "Who'd you use? In your paper. Who'd you use?"

"Mainly Foucault," said Alan. "But I brought in Prejean and others."

"Good. So you really did enjoy that lecture."

Last week the chaplain had taken him to see Sister Prejean speak at a local parish. It wasn't so much a lecture as a rally in support of getting rid of the death penalty and suppressing the politicians who favored it. Alan mostly agreed with her and the chaplain, but he still hesitated in some cases.

"Yeah," said Alan. "It was terrific."

"She really gets it. She's dead on with the slowness of our throwaway culture. Just look over there." The chaplain nodded to a wall where a trash bin and recycle bin stood side by side. Above the recycle bin a sign said PLEASE RECYCLE CANS. "If only we'd move a step further and start recycling people too."

"Yeah," said Alan. And then he asked, "How long do you think it will be until Craig is executed?"

"Years," said the chaplain. "Probably many years."

The two returned to the office and prepared to enter the jail floors. Alan took his wallet and keys out of his pockets and put them in his desk drawer, and he put his hand to his chest to make sure his ID badge was still clipped to his shirt pocket. The chaplain phoned down and asked for a deputy to greet them downstairs.

"Give me your hands," said the chaplain.

Alan reached out and let the chaplain take his hands. They always prayed before entering the jail.

"Lord," said the chaplain, "bless our time among those you've called us to comfort. Grant us the wisdom to speak when we have no words to say, the strength to shine when our surroundings seem so dim, and the patience to listen to those who so desperately need to be heard. Endue your ministers with righteousness to the glory of your name. 'Their sound is gone out into all lands, and their words into the ends of the world.' Amen."

"Amen," said Alan.

The pair gathered the four boxes of books that Alan had packed and made their way back to the ground floor. They set them beneath the service window and awaited the arrival of a deputy.

"Jean?" said the chaplain.

"One's on his way, Chaplain," she said.

"Thank you," he said. Turning to Alan, he said, "You shouldn't have to go through this every day."

Like the deputies, the chaplain could enter and exit the jail as he wished. But Alan always had to be checked. Moments later a deputy emerged from the east side of the window.

"You're taking all these boxes?" he said, looking at Alan.

"Yes," said the chaplain. "We are."

"He has to empty them," said the deputy. "Empty them out for me," he said to Alan.

"Is that really necessary?" said the chaplain.

"Yes," he said. "Standard protocol. You know that."

Alan started unloading the books rubber banded with the post-it notes on them.

"You by yourself," the deputy said to the chaplain, "carrying one box. We don't worry about that. But you know we have to check this. It's nothing personal."

There were many times other deputies let Alan right into the jail with boxes stacked to his chin without making him unload them. Now the boxes were empty, and the book stacks were all around the floor. The deputy surveyed the stacks, occasionally grabbing a book and bending it, then nodded at Alan, and Alan refilled the boxes while kneeling on the floor.

"Pockets and shoes," the deputy said once Alan had stood up.

And this part Alan always had to do, pulling his pockets out and removing his shoes, then standing with his legs straight and arms held out. The deputy beeped his wand over Alan's limbs and front and back. The wand beeped at his ID badge, as it always did, and then the deputy holstered it and patted down Alan's calves.

"He's good to go," said the deputy to the chaplain.

"Of course, he is."

Alan sat on the floor and retied his shoes. The people sitting in the rows of chairs waiting for their behind-the-glass phone visits had watched the whole spectacle. Then Alan and the chaplain followed the deputy to the door on the east side of the counter, both of them with two boxes of books in their arms. The trio looked up at the camera, the deputy waved his arm, the large metal door buzzed and slowly opened, and then they walked into the small standing area until the door closed behind them. Then they stood in front of another door, larger and thicker than the first, and this one opened by sliding along a track, its steel wheels grating the track, inching the door to the side just wide enough for the three men to pass through before stopping, reversing, and then sealing them in.

Inside the ground floor, there was a control center and armament. Six deputies were always inside, visible in their cube behind clear bulletproof glass. They viewed every section of the jail on stacks of monitors, seeing the common areas, seeing the multipurpose rooms, the elevators, the cells of the inmates under surveillance, seeing the outside structure of the jail, even seeing inside the other smaller control centers on each floor. The only weapons in the jail were kept there in that control center, and they also had keys that very few people could check out, like the chaplain, that gave access to each floor but not to each block.

The chaplain checked out a set of keys from the control center, and then the deputy left them. The pair walked with their boxes to the back wall, where there were two elevators. These elevators did not have buttons. They had keyholes instead, and the chaplain set down his boxes and inserted one of his keys into the wall and turned it to call down an elevator. The elevator's doors opened, the two put their boxes inside, and then the doors closed them in.

"How are they divided?" asked the chaplain.

"You've got one through four," said Alan. "And I've got five through eight."

The elevator was big inside. At least twice the size of the standard ones in most hotels and office buildings. There were no mirrors. There were no ornamentations. Just blank walls. All metal. And a tall ceiling. Way up there with a camera looking down. And where one would expect to see the buttons with the floor numbers on them, the buttons Alan always wanted to push first as a kid—instead of those buttons, there were eleven keyholes forming a vertical line. One for the basement below, where vans could pull in and out to take in and give out inmates as needed. One for the ground floor, eight for the eight floors of housing, and the top one for the roof, where inmates had use of a basketball court and running track at scheduled hours each week. In groups for the nonviolent accused. Alone for those accused of significantly violent crimes.

The chaplain keyed the fourth and eighth floors. "After delivering the books, go and see Craig first."

"All right."

"And I also want you to see Hector today."

"Ruiz?"

"Since he's been in court, he's been craving a lot more attention. I've still got a lot of new people to see today. You go talk to him for a while. He likes you. Tell him I'll see him in a day or two."

"Sounds good," said Alan.

"And try to spend as much time with Craig as they'll let you. It's all right if you only visit those two today. We'll catch up." The elevator doors opened at the fourth floor, and the chaplain picked up his two boxes and stepped out. "Good luck getting around," he said.

The doors closed Alan in, and the elevator headed to the eighth floor. Once he stepped out onto the floor, he would have to rely on the deputies to key the elevator for him. The chaplain petitioned for Alan to be allowed to check out his own set of keys after he was cleared to do solo visits without the chaplain, but they wouldn't allow it. It was common for the chaplain to find Alan stranded in the jail, stuck in the opening section of a floor, between an elevator he could not call and the large blocks of cells he could see into but not open. If the deputies in each floor's control center were too busy to get him or were themselves in the cell areas with the inmates, then he would be stuck waiting until someone could help him. A regular day consisted of fifteen minutes of waiting on this floor, thirty minutes of waiting on that one, an hour even sometimes, and then, at last, having dropped off the book requests and having visited however many inmates he could manage, a final keying down to the ground floor, where he could exit the jail and head back up to the chaplain's office to gather his things.

Stepping out of the elevator on the eighth floor, boxes stacked in his arms, Alan approached the control center between the two blocks, set down his boxes, and waved to the black glass. He could never tell if he'd been seen, so he stood there a few feet away from the dark glass, waiting. Each floor had the same layout. After stepping out of the elevator, he'd have the cell blocks to his left. There was the west cell block, then the control center, then the east cell block. The deputies in the control center could look into both cell blocks and the hallway where Alan was waiting. The entrance to each cell block was closed by a sliding door with bars. Inside there were rows of steel tables with attached chairs, and behind the common area, there were two levels of cells that arched around the side view of the control center. If the inmates on either side had been out in their common area, Alan would have walked over to the bars and chatted with them. But everyone on the eighth floor was in his cell as Alan waited. The other side of the floor, to his right, when he walked out of the elevator, had two large multipurpose rooms. They were used for visitations, medical check-ups, and the strip-searching of inmates before and after their court hearings. Instead of bars, the multipurpose rooms each had a horizontal window that could be looked through from the main part of the floor where Alan was standing. The two rooms on this floor were empty.

The door to the control center opened and a deputy stepped out. "Just set everything down right there," he said, "and I'll distribute it at dinner."

"Sure," said Alan. "Thanks." He started separating out about half of the contents of one of the boxes. The deputy was heading back into the control center, and Alan said, "Could you wait a second and key the elevator for me?"

The deputy waited for Alan to finish sorting out the book requests, and he walked with Alan to the elevator and keyed it for him, and then he waited with Alan until it arrived, and then when it opened, he stepped in, keyed the seventh floor as Alan had asked, and then stepped out and walked back to the eighth-floor control center.

In this way, and in various increments of time, Alan navigated from the eighth floor to the fifth floor, distributing books in his gradual descent, chatting even with some of the deputies who had come to know him and weren't so abrasive, and chatting with some of the inmates who were out of their cells and in their block's common area together. When he had arrived at the sixth floor, the inmates from block M were out in the common area, and one of the deputies let Alan in there, the control center sliding the barred door open a couple feet, then closed again with Alan inside, and most of the men were sitting at tables playing cards and chess, but some were doing pull-ups off in the corners where there were horizontal bars set up, and others were doing sprints up and down the short set of stairs between the two levels of cells. And some men were chatting through cell doors with men from other letters—the non Ms—whose turn in the common area had either passed or not come up yet. And Alan set the one box he was down to on one of the tables, and men walked to him, saying—Hey young chaplain, you got something for me—and some said—Hey Alan, you got my request—and Alan told the men who didn't fill out requests to go ahead and fill one out. It has to be official, he'd said. Put it on paper. And to the inmates who wanted a visit from him or the chaplain today, he said that they would have to wait until tomorrow, that he was off to meet with someone leaving for Quentin, and they all knew who he meant without saying a name. They all knew more than he did. And so Alan stood by his box and the block M inmates expecting a Bible, expecting a new devotional, gathered around him, men in red jumpsuits, Alan in bland color, a circle of red around him, and he grabbed rubberbanded books, and he read his own handwriting off the post-it notes, calling out the names but not the numbers, Davis Mitchell (6-M-32), Rodney Griggs (6-M-48), Stephen Torena (6-M-13), Paul DeWitt (6-M-29), Luis Maravilla (6-M-29 also), and so on, until he was done with the Ms and left the other 6s with the deputy to give to the men still in their cells, and Alan resisted an invitation to a game of chess, which he normally jumped at, and he talked for a short while and caught up with men he'd seen once or twice, and he met a few new ones, and floor six was a mild floor in terms of offense, unlike floor five, and most of them would put short time in at the jail and not end up in a prison.

Alan stepped out of the elevator and into floor five. He held one box now that was less than half full. The west blocks of the fifth and fourth floors were where they kept the inmates accused of violent crimes or whose behavior had become violent since their captivity. He walked up to the control center and waved an arm to the dark glass. This time, a deputy came out right away.

"Just leave the box there, and I'll key you down," he said.

"I'd like to pull someone out," said Alan.

The deputy was clearly annoyed. His face stayed flat but he gave a short huff that let Alan know he just wanted him to go away. "Who?" he said.

"Craig," said Alan. "Cell 17."

"Can't do it today. He's on the roof."

"How long until he's brought down."

"Don't know. Could be a while. He's been given extra time."

"I'll wait."

"Listen. You can't see him today. When he's brought down, I've got to make sure his cell is clean and his things are packed. Should've been by earlier."

"But the chaplain said I could meet with him today."

"Can't happen now." They each kept staring at the other. "Is that all? I'll key you down."

Alan didn't know what to say. There was nothing he could say to make the deputy let him wait to see Craig.

"Well?" the deputy said.

"Hector," said Alan. "I'm supposed to see Hector."

The deputy shook his head a little and huffed again. "Fine," he said. Then he walked to a multipurpose room, unlocked the door, waited for Alan to follow him in, and then walked to the closet in the corner, unlocked it, pulled out two plastic patio chairs, locked the closet, and then went to exit the multipurpose room, saying to Alan before he locked him in, "It'll be a few minutes."

Alan sat down in one of the green patio chairs. They always seemed out of place to him contrasted against the mute colors in the room. Some of the multipurpose rooms looked beige to him, some light gray, and some could only be described as off-white, very far off-white, but off-white still. But they had probably all been painted the same shade, and it was probably the overhead lighting that caused the slight variations. This room looked kind of beige to him right now, or tan, whichever one is lighter. Sitting in the room waiting, he became aware of the lack of noise, not silence—since there was always a humming of some sort, whether electricity, or the elevator, or the sounds of talking traveling through a vent or along a wall or floor or ceiling—but a lack of noise, a lack of discernible sounds, and he became aware of the air, never really stuffy or stale, certainly never crisp or fresh, but just flat. Not stagnant or unpleasant, just flat. And he did sympathize with the deputies despite the rudeness of some of them because they had it tough too. Two of them were back there now, getting Hector to turn around in his cell, cuffing his hands behind him first, then opening his cell door and putting on the full waist chains, hands, and ankles attached to the waist chains as well as each other. The inmates looked like penguins walking around like that, feet taking little baby steps despite their legs' length, long arms forced to the side of the body, pinned straight to make their torsos rigid and clumsy. And that was protocol, for moving inmates who were in the west block on this floor, even for transferring them a stone's throw over to the multipurpose room. Always in waist chains. And the deputies hated putting them in them and taking them out of them when it wasn't necessary, and Alan felt for them, but these visits were necessary, and sometimes he had to remind himself of that. "This visit is necessary," he said, leaning forward in his green plastic chair, staring ahead at its empty mate in front of him.

There was a clattering outside the activity room, and then Hector was there in the hallway outside the window, and the same deputy opened the door and another deputy with him—they always had to escort these inmates in pairs—guided Hector into the room, and then they both helped him into the chair so that the flimsy plastic didn't fall back when he plopped in.

"We'll be back in twenty minutes," said the first deputy. Twenty minutes sometimes meant ten minutes or thirty minutes or something else.

"Thanks," said Alan.

"Thank you," Hector added.

"Oh," said Alan, "and can you take those off him." He pointed at Hector's hands, which pinched a worn Bible together.

"That's fine," the first deputy said to the second one. "He's seen him a lot of times. Only his hands."

And the second deputy unlocked Hector's handcuffs and locked them back to his waist chains without the wrists in them, and after both deputies left the room and locked the door behind themselves, Hector set the Bible on his lap and stretched his arms out in front of him and then stretched them to the far-off ceiling, and then he placed his hands on his head for a few seconds, his bent arms forming a triangle on either side of his head, and then he flittered his hands up again and landed them back on the Bible on his lap.

"Thanks for that," said Hector. "It's nice when they do that."

"Of course," said Alan.

"Where's the chaplain?"

"His plate is full today. He says he'll see you soon, though."

"I need more paper. Tell him I'm out of paper."

"We'll get you more soon."

"And pencils. They only give me stubs of pencils. They're worn to the nub. I can barely write with them."

About five weeks ago at a preliminary hearing, Hector got upset at his court-appointed lawyer, apparently thinking he wasn't doing a good enough job, and while he was in his waist chains, his hands unable to move more than a few inches, he took one of those short golf pencils and somehow stabbed him with it, thrusting the side of his body toward his lawyer, pinching the short sharp pencil between his fingers so strongly that when his hip and hand and pencil together rammed into the lawyer's side, the pencil pierced his skin between two ribs and kept sliding into his flesh until all three inches or so were buried in his side.

"And they don't give me enough time in the library," Hector went on. "I need to work on my case."

"I'm not going to talk to you about your case."

"I'm not asking you to. I just need to get to those law books."

"The waiting list is always backed up. Besides, you know I can't help you get in there any faster."

"But the chaplain can."

"That's not his job."

"You're right. . . . You're right," said Hector. "Hey, did you see the paper today?"

"No. I didn't."

"I heard I was in there again. One of the other guys in the hole got a hold of the paper when he was let out for his forty. He told me through my door that I was in there. But then his time was up and when they put him back he took the paper to his cell. Not cool, you know. So now I've got to wait about four more hours until my forty comes again. And then I'll go to his door and ask him what it says. To see what they're saying about my case."

"I see," said Alan. "I'm afraid I didn't have time this morning to read it. I don't always get to it. Usually just on the weekends." The men looked at each other while silent for a moment. In the last half year, Alan became good at making prolonged eye contact with people. He was terrible at it before—talking to a professor during office hours, talking to a girl on a date—the context didn't matter. He was just bad at it, saying a few things, then looking off to the corner of the room before being able to look at the person's face again. But not anymore. Here he was, in a maximum security jail, locked in a room with a man convicted of and certainly guilty of killing two people, torturing two people, and Alan stared at his dark brown eyes, and Alan saw his thick black beard in his lower peripheral, and he remembered that he too had a thick beard now after not shaving for the last few months, and he thought that if someone took a photograph of them—in black and white so that no one would focus on the red jumpsuit—that people might mistake them for brothers. But Alan was nothing like him. He knew he was like a lot of them in many ways. He could see that he was like so many of them. But not this one. Not this one. And staring at him and receiving his stare, Alan then said, "So how have you been holding up? With all that's going on. How are you doing?"

"I've been good," he said. "I finally have some peace."

"That's good," said Alan. "How so? What's changed?"

"I have something," said Hector. "I brought something into my room. Snuck it into the hole."

All of the inmates housed in the west blocks of floors four and five were kept in isolation. In prisons, the hole was where an inmate was brought for temporary isolation. Usually as a corrective. But here in the jail, there was no hole that someone would be brought to and later brought out of. All of the inmates in the jail facing murder charges were in the hole all the time. They were in their cells alone for twenty-three hours and twenty minutes a day. And each cell in those blocks was the length of one twin bed and the width of three, containing a toilet and a slit in the door where their food would be passed to them on trays. Their cell door would be opened for forty minutes, one at a time, and in that forty minutes they could wander around the common area by themselves, take a shower, talk to the other guys at their closed doors, make phone calls, and when the forty minutes was up, they were put back in their cell, alone, waiting twenty-three hours and twenty more minutes until they could get out again for a little more space. Besides court appearances, the main interruptions to the twenty-three hour and twenty-minute stretch were infrequent visits to the roof and visitations from the chaplain or Alan. To get out of the hole here, an inmate needed to be found not guilty or, more likely, be given a prison sentence and integrated into the appropriate population. But sometimes trials lasted months. Sometimes even years.

"What do you have in your room?" said Alan.

"It's here now," said Hector, lifting his Bible an inch off his lap. "I keep it in here."

The corners of the paperback were frayed, and the long edge where the book opened was black from constant thumbing. "What do you have in there?"

Hector flipped open the book and slowly pulled out a leaf, delicately placing it in a cupped hand as if it were some glass figurine or porcelain collectible. "This," he said. "This leaf. I got it yesterday."

Alan felt his muscles relax. "Oh," he said.

"While they were taking me back from my trial, it was on the basement floor. Downstairs. Right next to the van as they led me out."

"And they let you take it?"

"They didn't see! I bent down and grabbed it. Look!" He showed Alan scrapes on the knuckles of his right hand. "Even in these chains I grabbed it."

"And so this leaf is what comforts you?" asked Alan.

"Yes. Of course."

"How so?"

"Well I don't see a lot of natural things, right? So you'd think it would be the connection with nature. But it's not that. It's a connection. But one of understanding, you know? This leaf was taken from the one thing that gives it life. It's already losing weight and changing color. Already I can see the moisture draining from it. I see the green darkening. I feel the texture getting harder. Crisper, you know? I like that this leaf and I understand each other. It has no choice but suffering. Withering. But it still is nice to look at now, isn't it? Still pretty, I suppose. I guess I'm jumping the gun with thinking about what I know it will turn into."

Alan knew better than to point out that Hector himself had caused his separation from the outside world. There was nothing natural about his falling into this place, his cell, this room, where he sat there holding that leaf like that. "That's good," said Alan. "That's good if this identification comforts you. You need comfort. And it has you thinking. That's for sure. It has you thinking about the states of things."

Hector placed his leaf back in his Bible, and Alan asked him what books he had been reading in it, and for ten minutes or so Hector flipped back and forth between dog-eared pages, asking Alan a question about something in one of the psalms, then something in *Philippians*, then back to another psalm, and Alan did his best to give the right kind of answers to a mind like Hector's until a tapping on the window interrupted them and a deputy unlocked the door.

Hector stood up, and Alan stayed seated. "Tell the chaplain to bring me paper," Hector said.

"I will."

"And pencils. I need pencils."

"I will."

"And tell him to see me soon. And you too."

"You'll see him next. It might be a few days for me."

"That's good. Thank you. That's good."

The deputy opened the door and told Hector to stay put and Alan to come out first. Alan got up and shook Hector's hands with his two hands as if they were still cuffed. Then he walked out and the deputy locked in Hector, who started waddling around the almost empty room in his ankle cuffs, mumbling something that Alan couldn't hear on the other side of the glass.

The chaplain stood at the other end of the floor's center aisle, near the second multipurpose room. He waived Alan over, and Alan met him there and saw Craig behind the glass sitting in the other room.

"I convinced them to give you five minutes," the chaplain said.

"Thanks," said Alan.

"You'll need to be quick. Just enough time to say your goodbyes."

"Okay."

"I'll wait for you here and we'll go out together."

A deputy unlocked the door to the second multipurpose room and motioned Alan to go in. Alan entered the room, and the deputy said, "Five minutes," and then locked the door behind him.

Craig was sitting in one of the two plastic chairs the deputy must have taken out of the closet, and then Alan sat in the chair across from him and scooted it in closer so that they were only a couple feet apart.

"It's good to see you," said Craig. "I didn't think I'd get a chance to say goodbye."

"Neither did I."

"Or to thank you."

"For what?"

"All the visits. Just being here. The hours of talking. It helps. I've appreciated it. I probably haven't thanked you enough. Or the chaplain."

"Of course," said Alan. "I'm happy to visit. I've enjoyed getting to know you. I always look forward to our chats." And Alan knew that part of his fondness for Craig was owed to the fact that he looked so much like his uncle—the same big square glasses, the same shade of brown behind them, the same out-of-control eyebrows, the same graying hair though they were both only in their forties, the same stubble pattern, and a similar cleft in his chin, though his uncles was deeper, but he had the same calloused hands from his hours of honest work, and he was also roughly six feet tall in the times Alan had seen him standing. But his fondness for Craig went beyond his welcoming appearance, certainly, but there's no doubt the likeness was part of it, especially during the early visits when Alan still wasn't sure how to handle his new role.

"Before I forget," said Craig, "let me give you my ma's address. In case you have trouble writing me at Quentin." With his hands cuffed to his waist chains, he scrunched his shoulders low and twisted his body a bit, a straining wrist and hand feeling into the front pocket of his jumpsuit. He managed to pinch a folded piece of paper out, removing it with thumb and pointing finger, then offering it to Alan a few inches from the center of his body, stretching the paper out as far as he could.

Alan reached in and took it. "Thank you," he said. "How is your mother anyway?"

"Oh, she's great. God bless her. She visited me on . . . Tuesday. That's when she's allowed now. It used to be Wednesdays. But now she's here on Tuesdays. Not here here. Like what you guys do. But downstairs. In those phone booths behind the glass. This is nicer. I wish I could see her like this. But I saw her then. On Tuesday. And called her yesterday. It'll be hard not having her around."

"She'll drive up to see you."

"She will. She'll make the trip. But it's a ways. There's the gas. And she still works. But she'll make the trip sometimes."

Alan nodded.

"And things being the way they have to be," Craig went on, "this is all for the best. If I'm not getting out, I don't want to stay here anyway. You know I've been thinking about what you said some time ago, about why Jesus had disciples. Remember I asked you about, Why these guys? Why even have disciples? Because they keep screwing things up. Or not quite getting it. You said they couldn't contribute anything with their minds really. In terms of guidance and advice. Do you remember what you said? You said companionship."

"That's right," said Alan. "I remember."

"And I've always liked that. It's not for guidance. Not for intelligence. Not even for protection. It's to have people around. Because he loved them. And he was human and needed to be around people. He got lonely like all of us. I can't imagine it. God as Jesus getting lonely. Wanting to have companionship. It's so great. Because he really gets us, doesn't he? He can really relate to us all."

"He does. He truly does."

"And I guess that's one thing I'm looking forward to. I'm scared of the end result. I'm scared of that. But in the meantime, I'll get to be around people. I'll have that companionship. Don't get me wrong. I'm so thankful for you and the chaplain visiting me as often as you can. And I'll miss seeing you guys."

"Of course."

"But I spend so much time alone in here. And I need that companionship. And now that I'm never getting out, at least I'll be put back among people. Almost like being in the world again after being closed off from it. And not just among people. But getting more air, more sky."

"And how was your time on the roof?"

"Great. I really needed it. It's raining now."

Alan looked to the wall that touched the outside, but there was no window there to see rain, and of course he knew that and then he shot a glance to the ceiling, but there were many floors above them and no chance of hearing rain, and of course he knew that, but it seemed to his reflexes that if it was raining outside there should be some way of telling from in here. There could be a hurricane sweeping through downtown for all he'd know.

"At least it was raining when I was up there. More like sprinkling. But enough to soak into my hair after a while. Which felt good. And they were nice enough to give me a towel to use up there before they brought me back down."

"So what could you do up there if it was raining on you?"

"Well, it was light. Just a mist at first. I shot around on the basketball court. Did that for ten minutes I'd guess. And then I ran a few laps, but I stopped because I get tired pretty quick. My legs get tired pretty quick."

"It's the same with me," Alan said. Stupid thing to say, he thought. Stupid thing to say.

"Have you been up there?" Craig asked.

"Once. When the chaplain gave me a tour early on. I'm not allowed to be up there when any of the guys are out. So there's never been a reason to go back up. It would be great if I could shoot around with people up there."

"Yeah, that would," Craig said, and then after a pause he went on, saying, "You know how you can't see down or out but only up?"

Four concrete walls wrapped around the roof floor, stretching up at least twenty feet high, probably more, and there were two layers of metal fencing running horizontally above, sitting on the wall tops like a see-through lid on a box. Being on the roof still felt like being in a large room, except there was the sky instead of a ceiling, though the sky came down to the inmates all sliced up and crisscrossed from the fencing above.

"Yeah. I do," said Alan.

"Well, there's never wind up there. At least when I've been up there. But I found a spot where there was some. And I couldn't remember how long it had been since I'd felt the wind. I'd stopped running, and I started walking along the walls, and by now there was a steady sprinkle falling, and then this breeze hit my face. And it stopped when I took my next step. So I backed up and it was still there. This soft wind that just kept coming, kind of shooting straight down on my head. I got on the ground on my back and scooted down until the breeze was on my face, and I put my hands behind my head as a pillow, and I swear it must have lasted ten minutes before it stopped. This wind coming right at me, and the sprinkling coming steadily but not too hard. And I don't know, Alan, but I tell you, it just seemed like God was giving me that. Like he was just giving me that moment. And I was shivering after a while, and I was getting cold and uncomfortable, but it was the kind of uncomfort that you just don't mind. Almost enjoy in a way. And I told myself, God's giving you this breeze, and you're not moving till it's done. And then when it was done, I stood up, and I wiped the water from my face, and I kept walking along the walls until they got me. I was tired. But whenever I'm up there I keep walking until they get me because I'm not always able to walk, you know, so I might as well do some walking while I can."

Then there was a tap on the window, and then there was the sound of keys.

"I didn't say enough today," Alan said.

"No, no. You're good. There wasn't time for a study. A goodbye in person. That's all I wanted."

"Good."

"And write me if you can. Write me when you feel like it."

"I will."

"And you'll get mail here?"

"Yes. But address it to Chaplain Castillo. Then put for Alan in parentheses."

A deputy told Alan to exit first, and Alan and Craig shook hands, four together, and Alan stepped into the floor's main opening and met the chaplain near the elevator. The two deputies then brought Craig out of the activity room, one on each side, and one of them said to the chaplain, "Don't key the elevator yet," and then they stood before the opening of the west block, and behind the dark glass of the control center, another deputy must have pushed some button or pulled some lever because the barred door started sliding, and then it stopped at the shoulder widths of the trio of gray, red, gray, and then the deputies and Craig stepped into the block's common area, and the barred door slid closed, and then the chaplain keyed the elevator.

After Alan had returned to the chaplain's office to put on his coat and place his keys and wallet back in his pockets, after he had grabbed his bag and umbrella, after he had signed out downstairs and returned his ID badge for his license, having already said, See you tomorrow, to the chaplain, after all that, he boarded the 82-line heading from downtown to East Oakland, and it was dark outside, and Alan was ready for spring to approach, when it would be lighter at this hour, when his internship would be ending and he'd get back to his coursework, and he sat in one of the blue bus seats because there was space, but he'd been sitting all day, sitting, waiting, listening, talking, sitting, waiting, and he felt like standing, so he stood, and he felt like walking, so he hopped out of the bus's back doors while the stopped bus was still accepting people, and he lived miles away, but he headed in that direction, and all around him there were signs of life, buzzing neon signs, cars, taxis, passersby passing by, here and there, darting like flies going their short distances, but he seemed invisible to it all, and he walked quickly, his bag looped around his shoulder and chest, his umbrella still attached to the top, unopened because it wasn't raining now, unopened because Alan did not need shielding from the rain, and he would like to feel rain now anyway, would like to be drenched in this moment, but he was dry and the night sky above him was clear, and he was glad that his thoughts on Jesus's companionship meant so much to Craig, was glad that things he said were sometimes remembered and did real things, and he had also talked about chronicling that day, had also said that Jesus needed people around him to observe, to record his deeds and actions, to tell and then to write, but isn't it interesting how words are received, Alan thought, and isn't interesting how the right words stick sometimes and the less useful ones have a way of stepping aside, a way of letting the right ones trumpet a bit more clearly for this person or for that one.

acknowledgments

I'd like to thank the editors of the following journals for first publishing these stories:

Bayou Magazine for "Chrysalis"
Cave Region Review for "A Small, Distant Thing"
Chiron Review for "Some Substantial Thing"
Gravel Literary Journal for "In a Laundromat in Long Beach"
Noctua Review for "His Early Paintings Looked Like Things"
Overtime for "Into the Ends of the World"
Palooka for "The Butcher's Tale"
Posit: A Journal of Literature and Art for "Café"
Rosebud for "Story at Midnight"
Sierra Nevada Review for "Thursday Morning at A. R. Valentien"

I'd also like to thank Jonathan Apgar for the incredible drawing he made for the front cover; I'd like to thank Stephen Cooper and the rest of the MFA in fiction faculty at California State University, Long Beach; I'd like to thank my literature, linguistics, and poetry professors at the University of Missouri; and I'd like to thank my chair James Lu, my dean Gayne Anacker, and my colleagues in the Department of Modern Languages and Literature at CBU.

Most of all I'd like to thank my wife, Elizabeth, to whom this book is dedicated, our two daughters, my parents, my sister, and the rest of my family and friends for being constant sources of encouragement and companionship.

about the author

Derek Updegraff is the author of one chapbook of fiction and three chapbooks of poetry and translation. *The Butcher's Tale and Other Stories* is his first book-length collection of short fiction. His short stories, poems, and translations from Latin, Middle English, and Old English appear regularly in literary journals and anthologies, including *Bayou Magazine*, *The Classical Outlook*, *The Maine Review*, *Metamorphoses*, *Natural Bridge*, *The Raintown Review*, *Sierra Nevada Review*, and *Windhover*.

His articles on Old English language and literature appear in such places as *Oral Tradition* and *Texas Studies in Literature and Language*, and he is a contributing writer for *The Encyclopedia of Medieval Literature in Britain* (Wiley-Blackwell). He holds BA and MFA degrees from CSU Long Beach and MA and PhD degrees from the University of Missouri. He is currently an Assistant Professor of English at CBU in Riverside, California.

CPSIA information can be obtained
at www.ICGtesting.com
Printed in the USA
FSOW01n0110080916
24714FS